C000127793

LICENSE TO BITE

NEW ORLEANS
NOCTURNES

CARRIE PULKINEN

This is a work of fiction. Names, characters, places, and incidents are either the product of the author's imagination or are used fictitiously, and any resemblance to actual persons living or dead, business establishments, events, or locales, is entirely coincidental.

License to Bite

Contact Information: www.CarriePulkinen.com

Cover Art by Rebecca Poole of Dreams2Media
Edited by Krista Venero of Mountains Wanted

First Edition, 2020
ISBN: 978-0-9998436-8-0

Drinking blood sucks.

Governor's daughter Jane Anderson is used to getting what she wants. When a girls' trip to Mardi Gras thrusts her into the arms—and fangs—of New Orleans' hottest vampire, he gifts her with immortality, super strength, and a complexion to die for.

There's only one tiny problem. Jane faints at the sight of blood.

When Ethan Devereaux meets Jane, his cold, lifeless heart learns to beat again. Convinced she's his late fiancée reincarnated, he turns her, claiming her as his own. But when Jane wakes up dead in Ethan's attic, she's loud, obnoxious, and downright ornery. He doesn't know if he should kiss her or stake her, but one thing's for certain…

She is *so* not his long-lost love.

But Ethan turned her, so he's stuck with her. Jane has three weeks to learn the ways of the vampire and get her license, or she'll be staked. If Ethan can't help her overcome her aversion to blood, his undead life might also be on the line.

Join the supes of New Orleans Nocturnes as they lighten up the darker side of the Big Easy in this fun romantic comedy.

CHAPTER ONE

"I hate Mardi Gras," Ethan Deveraux grumbled as he stalked along the bank of the Mississippi River. It was cloudy, cold, and slightly damp, and while the weather had no effect on him physically, combined with the cacophony of drunken revelry, it made him ornerier than a werewolf with mange.

Six college-age women cackled, nearly tripping over themselves as they stumbled toward him, reeking of wine and sugary daiquiris, and he crinkled his nose. "It's impossible to find a decent meal anywhere near the French Quarter this time of year."

"Lighten up, young one." Gaston took one of the women into his arms, planting what looked like a passionate kiss on her neck, as her friends stopped to stare. The woman let out a moan, sliding her arms around him to grab his ass, unaware of the fangs sinking into her neck —and the meal she provided for the vampire—before he pushed her away.

"Can I at least get your number, sweetheart?" she drawled, rubbing her neck where Gaston had bitten her.

Not even a scratch remained in the spot he'd pierced with his fangs.

"I'm not looking for a regular meal, *ma chère*. Just a snack." Gaston winked and turned toward Ethan. "She's better than decent. I'm sure her friends are too."

Ethan shook his head. "No, thanks. Have a nice night, ladies, and be careful out there."

The woman's mouth dropped open at the rejection, but her friends linked arms with her and dragged her away.

Staring out over the muddy river, Ethan took in the peaceful scene, trying his best to ignore the vexatious festivity behind him. Artificial lights dotting the suspension bridge stretching from the east to the west banks of the river cast an orange glow on the dark water, and a bird of prey silently swooped down from the sky, snatching a rodent from its hiding place in the brush—much like his mentor had done to the unsuspecting drunk woman. Like Ethan would do to someone sober before the night ended. He shuddered.

The unmelodious noises behind him contrasted with the picturesque view of the river. Out of tune instruments blasted out something that was supposed to sound like jazz, and the shouting and laughter of dozens of inebriated partiers grated in his ears like sand between his butt cheeks.

Why had he agreed to come here this evening?

"You've got a little…" Ethan wiggled a finger at the corner of his sire's mouth, where a drop of red marred his otherwise perfect pale skin.

Gaston chuckled. "Whoops." He licked the blood from his lip as he smoothed his dark hair back, closing his eyes and swaying slightly while a vampire Ethan didn't recognize stalked toward them.

A long black trench coat flapped around the man's ankles, revealing pinstriped pants and polished black shoes. He wore a bowler hat, and wispy blond hair splayed around his ears. "Pardon me, gentlemen," he said with a British accent. "I need to see your license and identification, please."

"*My* license?" Gaston stepped toward the man, puffing out his chest like a pissed-off peacock. "Have you no idea who I am? I've been in New Orleans as long as it's been a city."

The man swallowed hard, but he held his ground. "You bit within the city limits; therefore, it's within my jurisdiction to require proof of licensure."

"I did no such thing." Gaston flicked his wrist dismissively. "You've no proof."

"On the contrary, I have the evidence right here." He flashed his cell phone and tapped the screen, revealing a video of Gaston and the woman.

"Hell's bells and buckets of blood, I despise this new-fangled technology." Gaston crossed his arms, lifting his chin defiantly. "Who are you? You don't work for the Magistrate; you have no power here."

The man flipped open a leather wallet to reveal the golden badge of the Supernatural World Order and a plastic card identifying him as Constable Watson. "Your dominion is under audit. I'm here to make sure World laws are being enforced properly."

Satan's balls. If the SWO was in town, there'd be hell to pay for anyone who so much as sneezed on a human without the proper paperwork. Ethan slipped Gaston's wallet from his back pocket and showed it to the constable. "Here it is. He's been licensed from the beginning. Registered resident of New Orleans."

"Give me that." Gaston snatched it and shoved it back into his pocket. "I'm the oldest vampire in Orleans Parish, older than the Magistrate himself. I identify to no one." When he tipped to the left, unable to hold himself upright, Ethan grabbed his arm, steadying him.

"You might consider limiting the number of drunken tourists you consume, Mr. Bellevue." Watson gave him a disgusted once-over. "You certainly live up to your reputation."

Gaston growled, and Ethan patted his back, tugging him away from the constable. "We'll just be on our way then."

"I need to see your license and registration as well, good sir." Watson widened his stance, clasping his hands in front of him and straightening his spine.

"He's with me." Gaston loomed toward the unshaken officer, and Ethan pulled him back.

"I didn't bite anyone."

Watson raised his brow and typed something on his phone. "You're not licensed, then? That is a problem."

Ethan blew out a breath. This was exactly why he didn't come to the French Quarter during Mardi Gras. As if drunken tourists weren't bad enough, every vampire constable within a hundred miles swarmed the festivities, hoping to catch other vamps behaving badly. And now the SWO had sent in their own troops?

"I have a license." He pulled his wallet from his pocket and showed the identification to the officer. "But if I'm not biting, I don't see why it would be a problem if I didn't."

Watson squinted at the ID and typed the information

into his phone. "Haven't you heard the new mandate?"

Ethan shook his head and glanced at his sire. Gaston rolled his eyes, threw his hands in the air, and stumbled toward a bench before plopping onto the seat.

"All vampires living within one hundred miles of a populated city must be licensed," Watson said. "The grace period ends tomorrow."

"And if they're not?"

"Why, they'll be staked, of course. Have a good evening, gentlemen." Watson tipped his hat and strolled away.

"Did you know that?" Ethan sank onto the bench next to his sire.

Gaston waved an arm. "It may have been mentioned at a meeting of the elders last month."

"Last month? And you didn't bother to tell me?"

"You receive the Magistrate's email newsletter, do you not? It's his first attempt at harnessing twenty-first-century technology. Rather bold, if you ask me."

Ethan clenched his teeth. "It probably went to my spam folder." Leave it to him to miss an email from the ruler of supernatural Louisiana. He'd have to whitelist the Magistrate's address.

"Precisely why he should resume sending paper letters. The post office is much more reliable."

"It's actually not." He fisted his hands on his thighs. "You could have mentioned the new mandate. It seems like a big deal, getting staked for not having a license, even if you're not biting."

"You have a license. Trained by the best damn vampire to ever walk this continent, I might add." He leaned his head back and closed his eyes. "You haven't sired anyone, so you've no one to teach. Our bases are covered. It's of no concern." He opened one eye. "You haven't sired anyone, have you?"

Ethan let out a sardonic laugh. "I never will." He couldn't even think about cursing another human to this endless macabre lifestyle.

"No harm done, then." Gaston straightened. "I'm thirsty. Let's find a tequila bar. I'm in the mood for some Cuervo-tainted O negative."

Ethan rolled his eyes. "We'd better get you home before the sun comes up, old man. You're drunk." He reached for Gaston's arm, but the senior vampire jerked from his grasp.

"I'm not drunk! You're boring. If I'd known what a bore you would be, I never would have turned you."

Ethan's jaw ticked. "If I'd known what a drunk you were, I never would have let you." He ground his teeth, quelling the ancient memories. "You promised to end my suffering." Now, he'd have to live with the pain for all eternity.

"And I did." Gaston rose to his feet. "You were a lonely, miserable wretch when I found you. You were out of your mind, nearly killed when you stumbled into traffic, and if I hadn't been the one who'd run you over, you'd be an invalid now. Or dead."

"You should have let me die."

"But you wanted to live." He took Ethan's face in his hands. "I gave you a choice, and you chose life, my friend. It's a gift. Embrace it."

He looked into his sire's ice-blue eyes, and the memory of that fateful night twenty-five years ago came into crisp focus. Gaston was right. He didn't want to die then any more than he wanted to now. He'd only wanted the pain to stop.

Gaston patted his cheek. "I can ask the Magistrate for permission to stake you, but I've grown rather fond of you."

Ethan sighed, resigned. "I don't want to die."

"That's my boy." Gaston wrapped an arm around his shoulders and guided him down the riverbank, toward Jackson Square. "The emotional pain will heal with time. You're young, and you have your entire undead life ahead of you. Now, how about that tequila shot?"

Ethan chuckled. "One more, and then we find a meal who hasn't drunk her body weight in liquor."

"Deal. Although, I'm suddenly in the mood for Irish whiskey."

He followed Gaston's gaze toward a tall redhead tugging her reluctant friend down a side street toward an Irish bar. "Whiskey it is, then."

The place was packed, as were all the bars near Bourbon Street this time of year. The final parade of the evening had ended hours ago, giving the humans plenty of time to get shit-faced and the vampires a smorgasbord of unsuspecting victims. Mardi Gras and New Year's Eve were the only times a vampire was allowed to bite inside a bar. All other times of the year, they were required to have their meals in a secluded courtyard, an alleyway, or a bathroom stall, depending on how classy the vampire was.

"Vodka's nice too." Gaston followed a blonde onto the tiny dance floor, and Ethan leaned against the wall, crossing his arms and taking in the chaotic scene.

Patrons shouted their orders at bartenders, who rushed behind the bar, filling glasses and opening bottles, running credit cards and taking cash. An ass filled every seat in the room, but three-quarters of the patrons stood, laughing and talking with old and newfound friends.

Twenty-five years ago, Ethan might have enjoyed it. He liked to let loose every now and then, until the night he lost his fiancée, Vanessa.

He closed his eyes for a long blink, making room for the pain expanding in his chest. If he were honest with himself, he'd admit the ache had subsided over the years. But the pain was all he had left of the woman he'd loved, and he wasn't ready to let her go.

He let it resonate for another moment or two before opening his eyes and returning to the present. He'd never forgive himself for what happened to Vanessa, and he didn't deserve happiness. Not an ounce of it.

Shaking his head, he pushed from the wall and headed toward the dance floor. He'd given Gaston enough time to get his fill; it was time to go.

He maneuvered through the throng of people and made it halfway to his destination before a brunette stumbled into him. She fell backward, but he caught her by the shoulders, setting her on her feet with ease.

"Wow. Either you're really strong, or I've lost a few pounds since I last looked in the mirror." Her smile drew the air from his lungs, and though he technically didn't need to breathe, shock brought out his human instincts, making him cough.

She had long brown hair, chocolate eyes, and a sprinkling of freckles across her nose. Her voluptuous curves made his fingers twitch with the urge to run his hands along the peaks and valleys of her gorgeous body. The woman looked so much like Vanessa, his body seized. He stood motionless, staring at her as he calculated the time in his head. Could it be?

"Are you okay?" She touched his shoulder, and something inside him burned.

He composed himself, making sure his fangs hadn't extended, and smiled. "I'm fine."

"Yes, you are." Her friend, a tall blonde, handed her two shot glasses, and they both tossed them back, one after the other. The blonde smelled like warm cinnamon and cider. Like a witch. "You should do shots with us. I'll go get more."

"That's okay," he said, but she was already on her way to the bar.

"She's trying to drunk me...get me drunk." The brunette hiccupped and stumbled again.

"I'm afraid you already are." Ethan tapped a man on the shoulder and motioned with his head for him to give up his seat. The guy blinked, then got up without protest, Ethan's vampire glamour working its magic. "Have a seat. What's your name?"

"Jane." She sank onto the stool, rubbing her forehead.

"I'm Ethan."

"You're right."

He tilted his head. "I hope I know my own name."

"No, I mean I'm drunk. I don't feel very good." She held her stomach.

"Shots, shots, shots!" Her friend returned, carrying three glasses filled with bright yellow liquid. "I don't know what these are, but the bartender promised they're good."

"Sophie." Jane squinted at her through bloodshot eyes.

"I believe Jane has had enough." Ethan held up his hands, refusing to accept the drink Sophie shoved toward him.

"Fuck you." Sophie drank her shot and the one she'd bought for him. "Nobody tells Jane Anderson what to do." She handed Jane the glass. "Drink up, babe."

"Except for you, I see." Ethan crossed his arms.

Sophie gaped, and when Jane didn't drink her shot, she took the glass and set it on the bar. "Look, I don't know who you think you are with your looming presence and pecs you could bounce a quarter off of." She pressed her fingers into his chest. "Wow. Is your ass this tight?" She shook her head. "Who are you again?"

"Good evening, ladies." Gaston approached from the dance floor, and Sophie gave him a once-over, cocking a brow like she wasn't impressed.

"It's time to go home, Soph." Jane leaned her head on the bar. "I don't think I'll make it much longer."

"It would be an honor to escort you both." Gaston bowed formally, and Ethan caught a glimpse of fang as he smiled.

"Oh, no. That's not happening." Sophie crossed her arms and squeezed her eyes shut. "We can make it on our own. We can…" She swayed and opened her watery eyes. "Shit. I'm starting to feel those shots." She spun toward a trash can and spewed the alcohol and part of her dinner into the bin.

"Get them out of here." The bartender pointed to Ethan and jerked a thumb toward the door.

Jane rested peacefully on the bar, while Sophie leaned a forearm against the wall, dry-heaving into the trash can.

"I think I'm done." Sophie stepped toward Ethan and doubled over.

She was definitely *not* done. Vomit hit the floor, splashing onto his shoes, the sharp, tangy scents of alcohol and pineapple juice burning his nostrils. Jane's head slipped off the bar, and he caught her before she could fall out of her chair.

"You know how to pick them, my friend." Gaston touched Sophie's arm, and she yanked away.

"We're not going anywhere with you. C'mon, Jane." She reached toward her friend, and Jane slid off the stool, stumbling into Ethan again. They wouldn't make it to the door without help, much less all the way back to their hotel.

Gaston shook his head, making a *tsk* sound as he brushed his fingers to Sophie's temple, activating his glamour. "You will allow us to escort you to your hotel."

Sophie's expression went blank for a moment before she blinked, scrunching her forehead and turning to Jane. "Maybe we should let them take us. Our rental house is all the way on Esplanade. We can't walk that far."

"We don't need an escort," Jane said as adamantly as her current state of inebriation would allow. At least she had some of her wits intact, but how long would it last before someone took advantage of her vulnerability?

Ethan wiped his shoes with a napkin as Gaston gestured with his head toward Jane, but he hesitated to use his glamour. She, and this entire situation, reminded him so much of Vanessa, he wasn't sure his undead heart could handle being so close to her.

But he had to see these women to their hotel. If he could get them back safely, maybe he could atone for his sins. He slid his fingers into her soft, dark hair, focusing his magic to ensure her trust in him. "We'll take you to your rental house. I promise you'll be safe."

Jane's face slackened, and a pang of guilt shot through Ethan's chest. He would have preferred she trust him willingly, but with the pair of bouncers approaching from the left and the manager giving him the stink eye, he didn't have time to woo her with his charm. Not that he had any to begin with.

He pulled her to his side, lifting her slightly to feign

the appearance that she could walk, and carried her out of the bar. Too many monsters lurked in the shadows of the French Quarter, most of them human, and he'd never forgive himself if anything happened to the women.

Especially since—judging by the way his body was reacting—this Jane could very well be his Vanessa reincarnated.

His body hummed at the thought, and his fangs instinctively elongated, his mouth watering with the desire to taste her. If she'd been sober, he wouldn't have been able to help himself, but he'd spend eternity rotting in hell before he'd ingest another drop of alcohol.

"Keys, Gaston." He held out his hand as they approached his sire's jet-black Maserati Quattroporte in the parking lot.

Gaston hit the key fob, unlocking the car, but he kept the keys clutched tightly as he lowered Sophie into the back seat. Ethan settled Jane in the front passenger side and buckled the seatbelt across her lap before zipping over to the driver's door and blocking Gaston's entrance.

"Step aside, young man," Gaston said.

Ethan held out his hand again. "Keys."

"You, sir, are mad as a hatter if you presume I'll allow you to drive Genevieve. She's the only bit of modern technology worthwhile in this day and age."

"And you're batshit crazy if you think I'm letting *you* drive." He snatched the keys from Gaston. "This was part of the deal. You bring Genevieve into the city, but *I* drive her home, remember?"

Gaston narrowed his eyes. "Even drunk out of my mind, my senses are a hundred times sharper than a sober human's."

"I don't care."

"You really aren't any fun at all, my friend." He touched a fang with the tip of his tongue as he eyed Sophie in the back seat.

"Don't even think about drinking from her. We promised to get them home safely."

"Boring," Gaston sang as he sank into the back seat. "I'll oblige you this one. I'm still rather full from the bar, and I'm not sure what kind of magic she possesses. If she belongs to the coven, I'd hate to break our truce." He gently shut the door, running his hand along the leather armrest, caressing his precious car. "I do miss the taste of witches."

With the slightest pressure on the gas pedal, the car zipped through the streets, cornering like it was on rails. Speed and power. It was a car fit for a vampire, much more appropriate than Ethan's sensible Ford Taurus.

Ethan's glamour had sobered Jane enough for her to give him directions, and she sat quietly in the passenger seat, grinning at him as he rolled to a stop in front of the rental house, a white, two-story Second Empire style with green shutters and a balcony. Jane had a disarming smile, and his overwhelming need to see her to safety convinced him this was fate. He'd been given another chance, and he would not fail this time.

"Shall we rid ourselves of the baggage and return to the fun?" Gaston slid from the car and carried Sophie to the front door.

Ethan rolled his eyes and helped Jane out of the car.

"Did he just call us baggage?" she asked.

"Ignore him. He's old and ornery."

She giggled. "I like you. You're funny. Sweet too."

If that were only true. "You don't know me."

"I'm an excellent judge of character." That had to be the glamour talking. She'd completely misjudged him.

He'd seen her home safely tonight, but even through the alcohol, the scent of her blood sang. She'd be a temptation for any vampire who got near her, and the thought of another person's fangs piercing Jane's neck made his muscles crawl beneath his skin.

He couldn't let anyone else have her, so, brushing his fingers across her forehead, he marked her. The temporary magic would glow in her aura for a week, making her off-limits to any other vamps while her body replenished her blood supply. Some of the SWO regulations had their merits.

As he pulled his hand away, something in his core snapped, like a glow stick cracking and coming to life. Funny, he'd never felt that sensation before. Then again, he was supposed to drink from her *before* he marked her. It had been against the law to mark humans without consuming their blood for the past hundred years, ever since some asshat decided he wanted every woman in New Orleans for himself and went around marking them all, leaving the rest of the vamps to fight over the men.

Still, it was a minor law to break, and it wasn't like anyone would find out. He scanned the sidewalk for signs of the British constable just to be sure.

No one saw him do it, so no harm done.

By the time he walked her to the porch, Gaston had returned to the car and laid on the horn. *Impatient bastard.*

"Goodnight, sweet Jane." He kissed her hand, and the light that she'd sparked inside him glowed a little brighter.

"Thank you. You're a good man." She smiled and closed the door.

CHAPTER TWO

"I can't believe how badly my head hurts." Jane stared into her café au lait and gingerly pressed her fingers against her temples. It was two o'clock in the afternoon, and she finally felt well enough to venture out of her room. They'd waited in line half an hour to get a table under the famous green and white awning of Café Du Monde, but the nausea churning in her stomach killed her appetite for the beignets she'd been dying to try.

"It feels like I'm giving birth to a bowling ball through my nose. Are my nostrils dilated? I think it's crowning."

"I can't believe we got in a car with two strange men and let them take us to our house." Sophie bit into a beignet, and sugar rained down on the table. "They could have murdered us."

Jane pressed her thumb between her eyes to counter the pressure in her skull. "I know. What were we thinking?"

"We weren't."

She sank deeper into her chair. Her memory of the events that led up to meeting the men was a blur, but the car ride back to their rental house remained vivid in her mind. She couldn't explain why she'd let her guard down, aside from drinking way too much, but the man had been sweet, nothing but a gentleman. "At least they turned out to be nice guys. Especially the one who drove."

"We got lucky."

"Damn lucky. I wish I could remember his name."

"I'm surprised you remember anything." Sophie sipped her coffee. "You were trashed."

How could she forget a man like that? He stood half a foot taller than her, which made him at least six-foot-three, and he had the kind of wavy, dark hair a girl could run her fingers through for hours. His eyes were blue…or maybe green…and his muscular arms and broad shoulders that tapered down into a narrow waist alluded to time spent in the gym. Nice view, but probably not much going on upstairs. A man that good-looking couldn't hold up his end of a conversation if The Rock himself was his spotter.

"You looked pretty cozy with his friend in the back seat." Jane arched a brow and immediately wished she hadn't when pain sliced through her skull.

Sophie laughed and then winced, resting her fingers on her temples. "The goth-looking dude with black hair in a man bun? You know me better than that."

Jane shook her head. *Damn.* They were both smarter than that. In their defense, it had been their first night in New Orleans, *and* it was Mardi Gras. Everyone went a little crazy their first time, but still. "That was pretty stupid of us."

"*Very* stupid. They could have been vampires."

Jane scoffed. "Not this again. Ever since you found out about your grandma supposedly being a witch, you've been harping on all this magic shit."

"I found her grimoire in Pop's attic." She crossed her arms. "She *was* a witch."

"So you found a book of spells. Big deal. You can't get any of them to work."

"Because *she* was the witch. Not me. Anyway, that palm reader said I'd find magic in New Orleans. It's just a matter of time."

"Right, well, vampires are about as real as your boobs."

Sophie's mouth formed the shape of an O as she clutched her chest. "How dare you insult my girls. They're real."

"I drove you to the surgery."

"They're *enhanced*, not fake." She grinned. "Like vampires."

Jane rolled her eyes. When she first told Sophie she was planning a month-long stay in the Big Easy, her friend had droned on and on about the secret magical societies in the city, as if witches and werewolves, and…God forbid… vampires actually existed. They hadn't been in town two hours yesterday when Sophie squealed like a stuck pig and ran inside a store that claimed to be run by witches.

The employees had been tight-lipped when she plied them with questions about shapeshifters and creatures of the night, which only made her more convinced they were real.

"You're twenty-five years old, Soph. The only monsters lurking in the darkness are of the human variety."

Sophie shrugged. "You never know. The green-eyed one kept looking at you like he wanted to eat you."

So his eyes were green. "If I'd known my head from my ass last night, I might have let him. He was hot."

Sophie wrinkled her nose. "His friend was way too slim and pale for me. I want a big, tanned, hairy guy to warm my bed. I've got to figure out where the werewolves are hiding."

"Good luck with that."

Jane's phone buzzed on the table, her brother's name lighting up the screen. "Ugh. It's Justin. They're bringing out the big guns if he's calling." Her other three older brothers had already called twice today, which she'd neglected to answer, but Justin knew better. Two years older than Jane, he was the only one who attempted to understand her. To treat her like an adult.

"You better answer it, or your dad will send the Texas Rangers out looking for you."

Jane grinned. "The baseball team or the police? I could learn to be a sports fan."

Sophie snickered. "Seriously, though. They're not going to leave you alone until you pick up."

Jane groaned and grabbed the phone, pressing it to her ear. "Hello, dear brother. What can I do for you?"

"Why didn't you tell anyone you were going to New Orleans?" He sounded resigned and not at all happy about making this call. At least he knew he was doing her wrong. No doubt their dad had badgered him until he'd agreed to do it.

"I'm fine, Justin. And how are you and Amy? Any luck in the baby department yet?"

He sighed. "C'mon, Jane. Don't make this hard."

She straightened her spine, despite the fact he couldn't see her indignance. "I'm sorry. I didn't realize I needed permission to live my life."

"It's a dangerous city. You know Dad worries about you."

"All fathers worry about their daughters. Most recognize when they become adults." She'd purposely kept quiet about the trip for this reason. Her dad would have done everything in his power to stop her from going. And as the Governor of Texas, he wasn't lacking in the power department.

"He saw your Instagram posts. Here, he wants to talk to you."

Her mouth dropped open at her brother's betrayal. "He's there with you?"

"I'm sorry, Jane."

"You traitorous bastard."

Shuffling sounded through the receiver before her dad's booming voice filled the line. "Jane, sweetheart, what are you doing in New Orleans unescorted?"

Her eye twitched at his choice of words. Resting an elbow on the table, she cradled her head in her hand. "My job, Daddy. I'm a travel blogger. It's what I do: travel and blog."

"I'm not going to argue about your so-called occupation. We'll discuss finding you a real job later, but you and Sophie need to come home right now. It's not safe there."

If her eyes rolled any harder, she'd have seen the back of her skull. "We're fine, and we can take care of ourselves. You raised a fighter, not a victim."

"I know you can defend yourself, but there are criminals there you can't even imagine. Two women alone in a city like that is asking for trouble. Your self-defense skills are useless against..." He sighed heavily. "Come home, sweetheart. You can blog about somewhere safe, like Friendswood."

She ground her teeth, quelling the urge to go off on her father. Justin or Jared, or any of her brothers, could travel to the middle of a war zone, and the old man wouldn't bat an eye. But Jane was a woman. Fragile. Less than. "I'm staying in New Orleans."

Silence filled the line, and Jane's heart pounded as she awaited his response. "Okay. Have it your way," he said, "but I'm sending Paul to keep an eye on you. If you don't have a spare bedroom, he can sleep on the couch."

Now he'd crossed the line. She was not a child, and there was no way in hell her father was sending a babysitter to look after her. "I don't need your bodyguard following me around, and if you send him, I will never forgive you. In fact, I won't come home for Easter. Good luck getting one of the guys to wear that awful rabbit suit on the Capitol lawn."

"Jane."

"No, Daddy." Her head pounded even harder. She was way too hungover to deal with this shit. "I'm twenty-six, an adult. You have to trust me and let me live my life."

"What would your mother think about you running all over the place and never settling down?"

Oh, he wanted to play the dead mother card, did he? He must have forgotten how good Jane was at this game. "She would think you raised a strong woman who can take care of herself."

He sighed again. The man always sighed around her, like she was the biggest disappointment in his life. "All right, sweetheart. But if you get into any trouble at all, you call me. Understand? No matter what it is."

"Okay. I will."

"I love you, Janey."

"I love you too." She mashed the "end" button and shoved her phone into her purse. "I'm going to strangle Justin next time I see him. I swear my dad acts like I'm an idiot."

"Do you think he'll send the babysitter anyway?" Sophie asked.

"He better not." Her phone buzzed, and a text from Justin read *Don't worry. I won't let him send Paul. Stay safe.* She flashed the screen to Sophie.

"Maybe we should skip the shots tonight?" Sophie stretched her arms above her head, dropping them on the armrests as if they were heavy. "Keep our wits about us better."

Jane clamped her mouth shut as the phantom flavor of those syrupy drinks crept up her throat, triggering her gag reflex. Okay, maybe she was an idiot every now and then, but she wouldn't let it happen again. "Good idea. I can hardly stomach this coffee. Excuse me, ma'am." She flagged the waitress over. "Can I get a shot of morphine in this?"

The waitress gave her a sympathetic smile. "The best cure for a hangover is a Bloody Mary. Tujague's across the street makes a great one."

Jane groaned, her stomach turning. "Don't even mention blood."

Sophie snorted. "There's no actual blood in the drink. It's tomato juice and vodka."

"I know what it is, but is alcohol really the cure for too much alcohol?" She shrugged. *When in New Orleans...* "Why the hell not? I'll try anything at this point."

They paid the tab and crossed Decatur Street toward the restaurant. A few tables lined the wall across from the bar, but all the chairs were taken, and not a single bar stool offered her aching feet relief from all the walking she'd done since arriving in New Orleans.

"Where are all the chairs?" She leaned her elbows on

the bar and propped one foot on the metal railing near the floor. "Can't a girl take a load off in here?"

The bartender finished pouring a thick green liquid into a fancy glass and nodded at Jane. "This is a standing bar." He ran his hand across the polished wood surface. "Oldest bar in America, in fact. That mirror is older than the country itself."

Jane followed his gaze to a massive antique mirror with intricate swirling designs etched around the edges. "Well, this is the oldest my tired bones have ever been, so we'll take two Bloody Marys to go and find a seat elsewhere, thank you."

"The restaurant is open." The bartender poured way more than a shot of vodka into each cup before filling it with a spicy tomato juice mixture and sprinkling in Worcestershire sauce and cayenne pepper.

"Ugh. No food," Jane said. "This will be breakfast."

He laughed and filled the rest of the glass with olives and pickled vegetables before passing the plastic cups to her and Sophie. "Here you go, two hangover cures."

"Is that a guarantee?" Jane paid for the drinks and took a sip. The vodka registered first, sharp and strong, before the smooth, slightly sweet tomato greeted her taste buds, followed by the slow burn of the pepper.

"Nothing in life is guaranteed." He winked before turning to the next patron.

Drink in hand—which seemed to be the standard in this city—Jane followed Sophie into the cool February air and bustle of Jackson Square. Maybe it was her imagination, but three sips of this miracle concoction, and her head already felt lighter, the throbbing easing into a dull ache.

Situated in the heart of the French Quarter, Jackson

Square boasted a central park area with a grassy lawn, manicured trees, and an enormous statue of its namesake, Andrew Jackson, sitting atop a cavalry horse. A paved pedestrian mall lined the fenced-in park, where local artists and street performers enticed tourists to spend their money on souvenirs and photo ops rather than alcohol. Smarter choices than the fortune Jane spent last night that left her with nothing but a massive headache and the memory of a sweet, sexy man who could have killed her as easily as he'd taken her home.

Sophie stopped in front of a dog lying on its back in the middle of the walkway. Beer bottles lay strewn around the pooch, and it had a hurricane glass tucked under its paw. It wore a dozen strings of Mardi Gras beads around its neck, and a *Beers, Boobs, and Beads* t-shirt lay next to a puddle of fake vomit. At least, Jane hoped it was fake.

"Aw. Look at this little guy. Can I pet him?" Sophie knelt beside the dog, and its owner gestured to a card-board sign giving information about the animal and permission to pet him.

Jane dropped a dollar into a tip jar and snapped a few photos of the scene. "This'll make a great article for my blog. How long can he stay like this?"

She gathered more information about the man and his dog, and by the time she finished the interview, she'd drained her drink. "Wow. This really was a miracle cure. I feel so much better. Ready for another one?"

"Not quite yet." Sophie threaded her arm through Jane's and led her past the St. Louis Cathedral and out of Jackson Square. "The parade starts at six, and I remember you saying something about wanting to get as far down St. Charles as we can, away from the drunks, to get the full experience. Every post you write on the trip can't be about us getting shit-faced."

"True."

"Besides, I'm supposed to be working too. If I'm going to expand my company across state lines, I need to spend a little sober time in the city. I'm a small business owner, and you, my dear, are Jane Anderson, travel blogger extraordinaire, social media influencer, daughter of the Texas Governor…"

"Party girl who blogs because she can't hold a steady job." Damn it, that phone call from her father was getting to her.

Sophie opened her mouth to protest, but Jane held up a finger and defended herself. "Blogging is a real job, no matter what my dad says. I monetized my website, and tour companies pay me to mention them on Instagram. My brothers handle the investments of my trust fund and all the boring math stuff. It's my job to have fun and share it with the world." She gestured grandly with the hand that held her cup, dumping ice onto a man's shoulder.

He spun toward her, glowering. "What the fuck?"

"Sorry about that." She cringed and brushed a piece of ice from his jacket sleeve. "I can be such a klutz sometimes." She plastered on her Governor's daughter smile and batted her lashes, thickening her Texas drawl. "No harm done, right, darlin'?"

The guy blinked, disarmed. "Yeah. No problem."

"Be a doll and toss this in the trash for me, will you?" She held the empty cup toward him, and though his brow furrowed, he took it, shaking his head as he walked away.

Sophie crossed her arms.

"What? He was headed in the general direction of a trash can, and he shouldn't have cussed at me. It's rude."

"One of these days, you're going to meet someone who's impervious to your magical man-taming powers, and he's *not* going to drop everything to be at your beck and call." She laughed. "That's the man you're going to marry."

"Psh." Jane waved off the comment. She became a travel blogger to get away from her father's and brothers' control, which obviously wasn't working out as planned. She wasn't about to invite another man into a position of power in her life. "I can't help it if I'm good at delegating."

She paused, peering up at an intriguing wooden sign hanging above a bar entrance. The words "French Quarter Absinthe" carved into the misshapen piece of reclaimed wood appeared black against the medium brown tone of the background, almost as if they were burned in. Such a fun aesthetic. "Have you ever tried absinthe?"

Sophie grinned. "Can't say that I have."

"Look. The bartenders are dressed like pirates. It's my duty to share a place like this with the world." She turned her back to the entrance, angling the front-facing camera on her phone just right to snap a selfie with the sign. "Perfect. Let's make this our last drink of the day, and then we'll head to the parade and get some food along the way."

"Sounds like a plan."

Jane strutted inside and slid onto a stool, patting the one next to her for Sophie to sit. The place was small and dimly lit, with a giant ship's wheel hanging on the wall behind the dark wood bar. A couple sat at the opposite end, engrossed in their own conversation, and rock music played softly from a speaker hanging from a wooden post. Otherwise, the bar sat quiet. Dull.

"We need to liven this place up." Jane slapped a hand

on the green marble countertop. "I'll have one of those absinthe thingies."

"Make it two," Sophie added.

The bartender, a woman in her mid-fifties with gray-blonde hair and dark eyes, handed Jane a laminated menu listing at least a dozen different brands. Jane scanned the offerings before focusing on the woman. She wore a black pirate's hat and a brown bar wench dress with a nametag that read "Sally."

"Hi, Sally. I'm Jane." She held out her hand to shake, and Sally accepted. "I have no idea what any of this is. What do you recommend?"

"This one's my favorite." She pointed to the fourth entry on the list. "It's got a mild flavor, but it still packs a punch."

"We'll take two of those then." Jane leaned toward Sophie and snapped another selfie while Sally set up the drinks.

She filled a glass urn with ice water and set a small wine glass on the counter, filling it with a bright green liquid. A concentrated beam of light shone from above the bar, illuminating the drink, and Sally set a sugar cube on a slotted metal spoon atop the glass. She turned a spigot on the urn, and chilled water dripped over the sugar, dissolving it into the drink.

"Impressive," Jane said as she accepted the glass.

Sally repeated the show for Sophie's drink before excusing herself to the back of the bar to slice lemons.

"Can't say I've ever seen so much flare go into making a drink." Sophie clinked her glass to Jane's. "Cheers."

Sadly, the show was a thousand times better than the result. "Ugh. This tastes like toothpaste." Jane bucked up and chugged the rest of the awful liquid—true southern girls never wasted alcohol—cringing as the weird, minty, licorice-flavored concoction slid down her throat.

Sophie coughed, pushing her empty glass away. "We paid twenty bucks for that?"

"Live and learn." Jane typed her thoughts about the drink into her phone to reference for her blog post later: *Great show. Disgusting drink. Do not recommend unless you like black jelly beans and mouthwash…together.*

"Ow! Shit." Sally clutched her hand, lifting it in the air and gesturing at the other bartender. "Grab me a Band-Aid from the back, will ya, Jess?"

Jane's gaze locked on Sally's hand, and she froze. A half-inch gash sliced across her thumb below the knuckle, and bright red blood oozed from the opening, trailing down her wrist. Sally grabbed a towel, wrapping it around the wound, but it was too late. Jane had seen enough.

Her head spun, the sensation of her own blood dropping from her skull to her feet making the room turn on its side. Her stomach lurched, her eyes fluttering as her vision tunneled and she tipped over, sliding off her stool.

"Whoa, Nelly. I got you." Sophie clutched her shoulders, lowering her to the ground. "Deep breaths. In and out."

Jane sat cross-legged on the floor, leaning forward and willing herself to stay awake. Sophie shot to her feet and returned with a glass of water, pressing the straw to Jane's lips. "You all right, hon?"

She sipped the water, pausing for the room to stop spinning before she replied, "Blood."

"Yeah, it's cleaned up now. Not a drop in sight. Come on." Sophie dragged her up by the arm. "Let's get you some fresh air."

Leaning into her best friend's side, Jane shuffled out of

the bar. The crisp afternoon air helped to clear her head, and within minutes, she felt like herself again…a little embarrassed, but no worse for wear. "Did anyone else see that?"

"Sally did, but she thought the absinthe knocked you out." Sophie rubbed her back. "Do you think you'll ever get over your aversion to blood?"

"Doubt it. My therapist tried, but all she managed to do was dig up the suppressed memory that triggered the problem."

"That time you walked outside the cabin to find your dad field-dressing a deer?"

She shuddered. "Poor Bambi."

They strolled through the Quarter, crossing Canal Street, the six-lane dividing line between the French and American sides of the city, where Royal Street turned into St. Charles Avenue. Chain hotels with floors soaring into the double digits were interspersed with tourist shops and fast-food restaurants along the busy thoroughfares, making it feel like they walked into a completely different city when they crossed the street.

They stopped at Serio's, a restaurant with a muffuletta to die for—who knew chopped olives would taste so good on a sandwich?—and Jane chased it down with a Dr. Pepper, while Sophie munched on a meatball sub.

After way too much walking, the evening sun bled into night, and they claimed a spot on the corner of St. Charles and Conery in an upscale, safe-looking part of the city—just to make her dad happy—to watch the parade.

The crowd was thinner this far into the Garden District, which was a good thing, but Jane's feet were barking like angry dogs by the time they stopped. She made a mental note to stick with sneakers for treks like this in the future. She'd save her knee-high stiletto boots for their less athletic excursions.

Marching bands sprinkled between the massive floats provided toe-tapping background music for the spectacle that was Jane's first Mardi Gras parade, and she caught enough plastic beads to match her body weight. With a thick mass of necklaces draped over her head, she let most of the smaller, plain throws land on the ground. A girl could only carry so many, and these krewe members weren't stingy with the good stuff. Thick strands with massive beads and plaster pendants were normal here. She didn't have to show her boobs for anything, not that she ever had, unlike the carnival back home in Galveston, where krewe members expected the spectators to put on the show if they wanted the good beads.

Jane was all about having a good time, but she wasn't about to demean herself for any type of prize. Respect was the key to success. She looked down to examine a throw shaped like a locomotive when Sophie elbowed her in the ribs.

"Hey, aren't those the guys from last night? The ones who took us home?" Sophie pointed across the street.

Jane squinted, her heart thrumming as she searched the faces in the crowd. "Where?"

Sophie pointed again and let her arm fall to her side. "I swear they were there a minute ago." She shrugged and returned her focus to the guy who'd sidled next to her. Sophie would be busy for the night.

His buddy nodded a hello to Jane, and if she'd felt like being a good friend, she'd have played wingwoman. But the possible spotting of the mysterious man from last night sent a little flush of adrenaline through her body, and she couldn't help but continue the search. If Sophie saw him across the way, he had to be there. He'd probably just slipped behind someone taller.

She stood on her toes, trying to get a better view, when the tiny hairs on the back of her neck stood on end. Her skin turned to gooseflesh, and her blood seemed to hum in her veins.

Someone was watching her.

CHAPTER THREE

E than's fangs elongated, his mouth watering with the urge to taste her. Jane's long, dark hair flowed over her shoulders, hiding her neck, but he could imagine the vein pulsing just beneath her creamy skin, the soothing sensation of her warm blood sliding down his throat, her naked body pressed against his as he made love to her.

His dick hardened as he watched her from the shadows, behind her now, since her overbearing friend had spotted him when he stood across the street. Though invisible to the human eye, his mark shimmered in her aura, adding to her radiance. He hadn't been this drawn to a woman since his sweet Vanessa died, and that could only mean one thing.

Jane *had* to be her.

"She is marked." Gaston activated his glamour, sending the giggling woman he'd just bitten on her way. "Is it yours?"

"Yeah." His sire should have known what his mark looked like. He dragged his gaze away from the beautiful woman. "I didn't bite her; I just didn't want anyone else to."

Disbelief flashed in Gaston's eyes as he stepped closer and lowered his voice. "Do you have any idea what you've done? This is forbidden. It's been illegal for two hundred years, ever since Willem created that uncontrollable hybrid abomination that went on a killing spree throughout the entire parish. They both deserved the stake, if you ask me."

Ethan ignored his sire's rant and cast his gaze toward Jane. She turned her head, rubbing the back of her neck, her eyes searching as if she felt his presence.

"You can't blame this on your spam container," Gaston droned on. "I'm certain I taught you this law."

"It's spam *folder*." Ethan drifted toward her, his sluggish heart beating at as close to a sprint as his undead condition allowed. She hadn't found him yet, but as soon as their eyes met, he'd—

"Oh, no you do not." Gaston grabbed his arm and yanked him into the shadows of a building. "I am far too sober to deal with this. What the devil have you done?" He thumped his forehead, and Ethan blinked, shaking his head.

"I haven't done anything."

"Your mark. She is *sensing* you."

This was fate. She was meant to be his, so why wouldn't she? "It'll wear off. No one will know I didn't bite her."

"Ethan, my dear son, you did not simply mark her as a meal. That's a mating mark." Gaston stepped back, peering at the crowd. "Satan's balls, you're an idiot. Go." He shoved him, taking him by the arm again when he didn't move, then running down the street toward the next intersection before dragging him into a yard.

With his back against the wall and Gaston's forearm pressed into his chest, Ethan watched as Jane drifted away from the parade, down the dark street toward them.

"Hello?" Her voice was music from her lips.

"It's not a mating mark." He struggled to go to her, but Gaston refused to release his hold. "It felt a little different when I did it, but I didn't claim her that way. It's not possible."

"Oh, it's absolutely possible, my friend, and you've done it. What in hell's name was going through that thick skull of yours?"

"Nothing. I didn't…" He didn't mean to. He'd only wanted to keep anyone else from having her. To mark her as his own. *Oh, fuck.*

"'Nothing.' Of course, because you were thinking with the wrong head. What's the modern expression I'm obliged to call you? Oh, yes. Dick for brains."

"It's 'shit for brains.'"

"Is it?" Gaston leaned into him until the pressure felt like his ribs would snap. Jane stood ten feet away. "Activate your glamour so she can't find you."

"But if she wants to—"

Gaston's pupils narrowed into slits, his fangs lengthening predatorily as a low hiss escaped his throat. "Do it now, or on my mother's grave, I will stake you myself."

Uh oh. He was serious. Funny how a little adrenaline could sober a guy up.

Ethan turned on his glamour full blast, blocking her from seeing or sensing him, and Jane stopped in her tracks, scratching her head before parking her hands on her hips. "Huh." She looked up and down the street. "I could have sworn I saw him."

She spun in a circle, then something in the distance

caught her eye. Her entire face brightened, and she cast a glance toward the parade, typed something on her phone, and then turned around, heading straight for Lafayette Cemetery #1.

With Ethan's hold on Jane broken for the time being, Gaston released him. "You need to remove the mark before anyone else finds out."

He drifted toward her, no longer needing the cover of shadow with his glamour concealing him from human eyes. "I'm not even sure how I marked her. I don't think I can remove it." And why should he? Accidents like that didn't just happen. It had to be fate.

"Do you have a death wish?"

"I'm already dead."

"*Un*dead. If you don't remove that mark before the Council finds out, you'll be *really* dead. Mate-marking a human is punishable by stake. You know this."

Well, shit. "Have you ever mate-marked anyone?"

"I prefer to sow my oats in the wild, an attitude I've been trying to instill in you, my friend. Now fix this."

"It really was an accident, man. I don't…" He blew out a hard breath. Damn it, he didn't want to remove the mark. "I think she's Vanessa."

Jane pranced across the deserted street toward the cemetery gate, her posture deflating when she found it locked. She rattled the chain, tugging on the lock before attempting to slip between the bars. Ethan smiled, admiring her tenacity.

"What in Satan's domain would make you think that?" Gaston cocked his head as he watched her snap pictures through the fence.

"She looks like her, doesn't she? Her hair, something in her eyes, her smile."

"Mmmm... Not really, my friend. Not how I remember her."

"You never knew her."

"I saw pictures."

"Which you burned fifteen years ago."

Gaston held up his hands. "I did you a favor that day. You'd been mourning the woman for ten years, and her energy couldn't pass on with that shrine you'd made in your bedroom."

"I loved her."

"And it was time to let her go. Tell me you didn't feel lighter—once you got through your murderous rage."

"I didn't speak to you for six months."

"And you felt better. I know you did, my friend. We're connected, remember?"

Ethan gritted his teeth, nodding grimly. It killed him to admit it, but he did feel a sense of freedom after his sire burned every trace of Vanessa's existence. Social media didn't exist back then, so all he had left now were the memories, and even those were starting to fade.

"I'll be a callous prick like you any day now."

"That's my boy." Gaston slapped him on the back and cast Jane a curious look. "What is she doing?"

Jane crossed to their side of the street again and stood with her back toward the cemetery, smiling at her phone as she snapped photo after photo.

"They're called selfies, old man." Ethan laughed. "I know I've explained the phenomenon to you before."

Gaston grimaced. "I've been drunk since then."

Jane sighed, chewing her plump bottom lip as she flipped through the photos on her phone. Seemingly unsatisfied, she lifted the device and resumed snapping pictures, stepping backward, closer toward the cemetery gates after each shot.

A car horn blared as a Toyota zoomed past, and Jane flinched but resumed her selfie-taking.

"She's not the sharpest stake in the pile, is she?"

Ethan smiled, unable to take his gaze off her. "She's perfect."

Gaston shook his head. "Remove the mating mark, and then I'll leave you to her. Do what you want with her, as long as…"

"She's alive and well and has no clue what I am. I know the rules."

Jane took a step backward. Then another. Right into the path of a jacked-up pickup truck. Ethan's stomach lurched, the sounds of crunching bone and tearing flesh clawing through his ears as the *thump, thump* of the tires sounded like the vehicle had done nothing more than hit a speed bump. She didn't scream, and with everyone at the parade, no one witnessed the accident.

The truck stopped for a moment before peeling out and speeding away, leaving poor Jane crumpled and dying —or already dead—alone on the pavement.

"Well." Gaston shoved his hands into his pockets. "Problem solved. Let's go find dinner."

"Jane!" Ethan ran to her, lifting her flattened body into his arms. The coppery, sweet scent of her blood greeted his senses like the smell of fresh-baked cookies straight from his grandma's oven. Her breath came in short, shallow pants, and her lids fluttered, her eyes rolling back so far he saw nothing but white.

With a burst of supernatural strength, Ethan leapt over the cemetery wall, landing gracefully in a patch of grass inside the graveyard. He laid Jane on her back, folding her hands on her stomach, and stroking her hair from her forehead. "Stay with me. I can't lose you again."

Gaston drifted down in front of him and dropped her purse and phone next to her before clasping his hands behind his back. "If you're going to drain her, be sure you're done before her heart stops beating." He tilted his head. "Better make it fast, or she won't have much blood left."

A burning lump of hot coal lodged in Ethan's throat as he gazed at his long-lost love, slipping away from him again. "How do I turn her?"

"Pardon?" Gaston held a hand to his ear. "This being sober nonsense is affecting my hearing. I thought you asked how to turn her."

"How?" Ethan's voice grated in his throat. "I have to save her."

"If I recall, when I tried to teach you this lesson, you swore on your still-living-at-the-time mother's grave that you would burn in hell for all eternity before you'd curse another human to this fate."

"I never said that."

"Oh, but you did. You can be quite the dramatic monarch." Gaston picked at his nails absently.

"It's drama queen, you relic. Now, are you going to help me or not?"

Jane gasped, and blood bubbled from her throat.

"Gaston…" Ethan growled through his teeth. "She's Vanessa. I know she is, and I can't lose her again."

"And damning her to darkness is the perfect way to show the woman you love that you care. What if she's not Vanessa?"

"I marked her. She's mine. Please help me save her."

"You're making a mistake, my friend."

Ethan trailed his fingers down her cheek, wiping the blood from her lip with his thumb. "I don't care."

Gaston shrugged. "Drink from her; absorb her essence and use your magic to form a connection. When you feel the bond tighten, stop. Then she'll need to drink from you."

She wasn't even breathing. He may have already been too late.

He pulled the mass of beads over her head and sank his fangs into her neck, sucking the delicious life force from her veins. Resting a hand on her battered chest, he instilled her with his magic until a connection formed, like a cord running from her core to his.

He licked the puncture wounds—vampire spit had magical healing properties—and her head lolled to the side.

"Time is not your friend." Gaston toed her limp leg with the edge of his boot. "Get your blood into her."

Ethan bit into his wrist, hard enough to tear his skin to delay his quick healing, and squeezed his forearm, working his slow-moving blood to the surface. As a drop gathered inside the wound, he pressed it to her lips, massaging his arm to encourage the flow into her mouth. "Come on, *cher*, swallow."

Jane didn't respond. The heavy weight of despair slammed into his chest, and he hung his head, leaning down to press a goodbye kiss to her forehead. As his lips met her skin, she swallowed, latching on to his arm and sucking with the force of a top-of-the-line Dyson. Her lids flew open, her pupils constricting into pinpoints as her body's injuries began to heal.

"Don't let her drain you." Gaston placed a heavy hand

on his shoulder. "You have to be functioning when she awakens."

Ethan pried his arm from her vacuum grip, and she sat up, her wide eyes blinking as she took in her surroundings. She looked at him and tilted her head. "I remember you."

His chest tightened, a strange flitting sensation forming in his stomach as he held her gaze.

Bringing her fingers to her lips, she wiped the blood from the corner of her mouth and peered at her hand. Her brow furrowed before her eyes rolled up, and she flopped onto her back, unconscious.

Ethan looked up at Gaston. "Is that…normal?"

Gaston shrugged and lifted her shirt, examining her injuries. "You were conscious a bit longer before the death sleep took over, but she's healing. She should awaken at dusk tomorrow."

Ethan yanked her shirt down, covering her torso. "What do I do now?"

Gaston chuckled. "Take her home and hope to hell she's the woman you think she is. You're stuck with her now."

CHAPTER FOUR

What on God's green Earth did Jane drink last night? Hell, what did she *do*? She squeezed her eyes shut, rolling over and willing herself to go back to sleep. Her throat felt like the Mojave Desert on an August afternoon, complete with a prickly little cactus growing at the base of her tongue. She swallowed, and another cactus cropped up just below the first one.

She moaned, the sound grating in her esophagus, and someone in the room stirred. Had she and Sophie passed out in the living room of their rental? They'd only been in New Orleans two nights, and they'd managed to get shit-faced both times. They needed to slow down.

Jane rolled onto her back and rubbed her face, still afraid to open her eyes. These sheets weren't nearly as soft as the ones on her bed, and the room had a musty scent to it, while the rental house normally smelled like peach pie.

Oh, dear Lord, she never made it home last night. The person sitting on the mattress next to her wasn't Sophie. *Think, Jane. Think. Who did you pick up?* She racked her brain for a memory of what drink could have fucked her up so badly and what man she could have followed home, but aside from the nasty absinthe she'd had that afternoon, she couldn't recall a single shot.

Well, Jane, you made this bed…and probably did a helluva lot more than lie in it. Time to make nice with the bear you poked and get the hell out of Dodge.

She pried her eyes open, expecting the morning—or possibly afternoon—sun to stab into her pupils like daggers, triggering the massive headache she was sure to have, but darkness engulfed the room. Her vision adjusted quickly, and she found herself staring up at wooden rafters not five feet from her head. *What the hell?*

A lamp switched on, bathing the room in yellow light, and the dagger effect came on full-force. She expelled a breath of air, but with her throat so parched, she sounded like a spooked house cat guarding its favorite toy.

"Hi, Jane. How do you feel?" A familiar, smooth, deep voice drifted toward her, and the tension in her chest eased. If she had to spend a wild, drunken night with a stranger, at least he was a hot stranger.

She rolled onto her side and found him fully dressed in jeans and a dark gray t-shirt. He sat on the edge of the bed, his hands folded in his lap, nervous tension rolling off him in waves. A lock of dark hair fell across his eye, and he brushed it back, his biceps flexing with the movement.

Her stomach fluttered, and a warm, fuzzy feeling flooded out from her chest to her toes. *Damn.* The last time she felt this giddy about a guy was with Aaron Dicks, freshman year of college. That man sure lived up to his name, unfortunately in more ways than one. Her asshole meter functioned at full capacity these days, though, and this guy seemed okay.

"Jane?" His eyes held concern. Concern was a good,

nonassholish emotion.

"Hey." She propped herself on her elbow. Her clothes were still on too. *Weird.* "I didn't mean to hiss at you. My throat's dry."

He shrugged. "It's normal."

She laughed. "Women hissing at you when they wake up in the morning is normal?"

He pressed his lips together.

"Where are we?" She sat up, taking in her surroundings. Cobwebs clung to the corners of the rafters, and dust motes hung stagnant in the air. That explained the smell.

"We're in my attic. Jane, what do you remember about last night?"

"We must've had one helluva time to wind up sleeping in your attic. Did I do shots again? Sophie and I promised each other we wouldn't do shots this time, but I don't remember what happened after the parade. We weren't planning to drink anything."

Why was he asking her what she remembered? Could he not recall the night either? She sucked in a sharp breath. "Did someone drug us?"

"No. We weren't drugged."

"Oh, good. That makes me feel better, though I'm pissed at myself for doing shots again." Hold on, she was in this man's *attic*. Warm fuzzies or not, shouldn't she have been panicking or at least calculating a quick exit? Any woman in her right mind would be out the door the moment she found her shoes, but something about the quizzical look on this guy's face and the way his jaw ticked as his brow furrowed had her more curious than frightened. In fact, she wasn't the slightest bit scared at all. Lord knew she'd found herself in situations much weirder than this.

She slid to the edge of the bed, setting her socked feet on the plywood floor. "Be a doll and grab my boots for me, would you?" She pointed to her shoes and purse sitting in the corner.

"You didn't do shots, and your boots are within arm's reach." His face was so serious, she'd have thought he was going to tell her he gave her crabs or something.

Oh, God. There were quite a few somethings a lot worse than crabs. She stretched an arm toward her belongings, wiggling her fingers. When he didn't take the hint, she sighed and grabbed them herself before slipping them on. "Please tell me we used protection."

He blinked, confusion clouding his eyes for a moment before his brow rose. "We didn't have sex."

A sense of relief battled with the sting of rejection. She wanted to ask *Why the hell not?*, but if she'd been as drunk as she thought last night, maybe that was a good thing. He'd had two chances to take advantage of her now, yet he hadn't touched her. The fluttering in her stomach reached up to her chest, and she warmed to him even more.

"That explains why my clothes are still on." She tugged on the hem of her shirt, and her eyes widened as she took in its condition. A crusty, dark red substance was smeared across the front, and...was that a tire mark?

"Holy fuck." She looked at the guy, but she couldn't for the life of her remember his name. "John?"

He tilted his head, looking offended.

"Paul? George? Ringo? What's your name again?"

"Ethan." He blinked once, his dark lashes fringing emerald green eyes. Was he smoldering at her?

Judging from the way the flutter in her core had settled below her navel, his smolder was about to set her ablaze. Damn, he was hot. Good-looking and a gentleman, yet somehow, he'd gotten her into his attic. This didn't add up.

"Ethan. That's right. What the hell happened last night, Ethan?" She stood and knocked her head against a rafter with a smack. A quick, sharp pain sliced through her skull and dissipated just as fast. "Seriously, dude. Why are we in your attic? Is this some weird fetish? I'm usually down for just about anything, but I need to know what I'm getting into before I agree to it."

He didn't crack a smile. "What do you remember?"

So he wanted to play this game, did he? It seemed Mr. Serious watched a tad too many docudramas on the old TV. She had two choices: walk out the door now, look for a new vacation rental so he couldn't find her, and get on with her life…or sit down and play along.

She scanned the room for any possible murder weapons, but other than the mattress and a lamp, the room sat empty. Not that she was worried about becoming his next victim. In addition to her black belt in karate, Jane was an excellent judge of character, and not a single warning alarm had gone off in her mind since she woke up. Not to mention, the man could make her clothes fall off with a simple look, and Jane never fawned over men. There was something special about Ethan, even if he didn't have much to say.

Besides, she was dying to know how they ended up spending the night in his attic. "This is almost as weird as the time I woke up in Brock Johnson's grandma's panic room. Do you live with your parents?"

He arched a brow. "No."

"Wife? Girlfriend?"

"No."

"Okay, you win." She sank onto the edge of the

mattress. "I'll play your game, but only because the curiosity is driving me bonkers. Why are you looking at me like that?"

He pursed his lips, looking thoughtful for a moment and not at all pleased. "You're not what I expected."

"Well, you don't have to look so damn disappointed. I thought you'd be a little more exciting too. You know what? Never mind." Her tolerance for bullshit had reached its limit, so she rose to her feet, hunching over to avoid slamming her head into the ceiling again. "I don't even care how we ended up here. If we didn't have sex, then no harm done. I'm out."

Clutching her purse, she made for the door, but he shot to his feet and leapt toward it, blocking her exit faster than she could say, "Holy hell raisers, you're fast!"

"Hell raisers?"

"I don't know where that came from. Move. I'm leaving." She grabbed the knob, but he palmed the door, keeping it closed.

"You can't leave. It's still daylight."

"I sure as hell hope it is. Move." She tugged on the knob, but it wouldn't budge.

"I can't let you leave." His voice deepened like he actually thought he had some kind of authority over her.

"Fuck that. I said move." She shoved him—a smidge harder than she planned to, but the guy was trying to hold her hostage—and he stumbled, his eyes widening in surprise before his head smacked into a rafter. *Damn, adrenaline is something else.*

She yanked the door open, and the brightest, goddamn blinding light she'd ever seen sliced through the opening like hellfire exploding through a ground fissure. Her vision went solid white, and her eyeballs burned like they were melting out of their sockets. Her skin sizzled, and as she fell back on her ass, she could have sworn she smelled the aroma of burning flesh.

Ethan slammed the door, engulfing the room in glorious darkness, before he scooped her into his arms and laid her on the mattress. "I told you not to do that." Was he scolding her?

She blinked, her vision coming back into focus, her eyes, thankfully, still solid and in their sockets. Her face stung, and the sand content in her throat doubled along with the cacti. "Holy Mother of God…" The moment she uttered the word, a coughing fit racked her body, and it felt like she'd swallowed hot coals.

Gasping for breath, she curled into a fetal position, slowly getting herself under control. "Jesus Christ." Another coughing fit consumed her, and if she didn't know any better, she'd have sworn smoke escaped from her throat. "What the fuck?"

Ethan hung his head in his hands, muttering what she thought sounded like, "I've made a mistake."

Sitting up, she slid her feet to the floor. "*You* made a mistake? I'm the one who opened the goddamn—" Again with the coughing. She doubled over, nearly expelling a lung before she could breathe again.

"Rule number one: obey your sire. Your life is in his hands until you're trained."

"Obey my what?" Gripping the edge of the mattress, she chose her words carefully. "Back up a minute, Christian Grey. I don't know what kind of kink you're into, but Jane Anderson obeys no one. Got it?" *Whew.* She spoke a whole sentence without her lungs trying to make a break through her mouth.

He narrowed his eyes, and his jaw ticked, but he

remained silent, almost stoic. Something outside that door had nearly killed her, yet the only emotion he seemed capable of expressing was disdain.

She took a deep breath and let it out slowly. She had to keep her cool. "What just happened? Why did I feel like I was on fire?"

Ethan sighed dramatically, as if he were the one nearly burned alive by opening a door, and dragged his hands down his face. "You were hit by a car last night, and I brought you here to save your life."

Jane opened her mouth to argue, but the memory crept back into her mind. She'd been at the parade, and something had compelled her to wander down the street. She'd found that creepy cemetery with all the aboveground tombs, but the gates were locked. It would have made a sensational article for her blog. Her stomach sank. "I was trying to get a photo." And that truck had come from nowhere.

He angled his body toward her. "Do you remember anything after that?"

"I remember…" Her jaw trembled, so she snapped it shut. It wasn't possible. This wasn't a memory; it was a hallucination. He didn't float her over the cemetery wall, and he certainly didn't… She swallowed hard. "Did you bite me?"

"I'm a vampire, Jane. And now, so are you." He said it so matter-of-factly, like it was just a…well, a matter of fact.

A nervous giggle bubbled from her throat. "What?"

"Vampire." He bared his teeth and tapped a fang.

A goddamn fang.

"Oh, come on." She scooted away. "Those are prosthetic. Vampires aren't real." They couldn't be.

"Aren't we? You didn't take too kindly to daylight just then, and that was filtered through glass. Imagine what direct sunlight would do to you." He narrowed his eyes at her, giving her that full-on smoldering effect again, making her stomach flutter, and an annoying little voice in the back of her mind whispered that she should believe him.

But she couldn't. "That was… You put something out there to keep me in. A massive heat lamp or something."

"Do you really think I'd go to that much trouble to keep you trapped inside my attic? I could have just locked the door."

"Well…" He had her there, but still. Vampires? "Tell me the truth, Ethan. This isn't funny. Did Sophie put you up to this?" Her friend had been trying to convince her vampires were real since they started planning this trip. It wouldn't surprise her.

"Your friend is a witch, yet you refuse to believe in vampires?"

So it *was* Sophie. "I knew it. I knew that little tramp set this up. What did she tell you?"

"She didn't tell me anything. She smells like a witch."

Jane scoffed. "Smells? Tell me then, what does a witch smell like?"

"Like spices. Sophie's magic smells somewhat like cinnamon. It's faint, though. Is she aware she has powers?"

"Oh, come on. Cinnamon? Really?" She threw her hands in the air. "Tell me the truth, Ethan, and cut the vampire crap."

"I wish this wasn't the truth, but it is. Do you have a mirror? Your face still hasn't healed from the light. Look at it."

"Ha. See, I knew you were lying." She dug in her purse

for her compact, a smug smile curving her lips. "Vampires don't cast reflections." She flipped open the plastic container and looked at herself in the mirror. "Oh, my."

Her hair was a rat's nest, and mascara stains streaked her face, but the most disturbing sights were the bright red blisters on her cheeks and forehead. She tilted her head, staring as they shrank into nothing right before her eyes.

She caught Ethan's reflection over her shoulder, his expression unreadable. Her lips twitched, and she hesitated to open her mouth. If she had fangs too, she'd...

She smiled, and her teeth were normal.

Blowing out a breath of relief, she looked over her shoulder. "You know, you're so serious about all this, you almost had me believing you. I can see you in the mirror."

"Of course you can. Everything casts a reflection, even vampires. Unless we're using our glamour." He nodded at the mirror. "Look again."

She rolled her eyes and glanced in the mirror again. Wait a minute, that couldn't be right. She squeezed her eyes shut and opened them again, but her face was the only reflection she saw. She jerked her head toward him, but he hadn't moved from his spot on the corner of the mattress. She scooted closer, holding the mirror directly in front of his face, moving it to the side and all around him. Nothing.

"Holy shit."

"Believe me now?"

"How are you doing that?"

"Glamour. It's a type of vampire magic that allows us to go unnoticed among humans. It's why you didn't see me when you wandered down that side street last night, which wasn't the smartest thing to do in New Orleans."

"I never claimed to make the best decisions." *Damn.*

Maybe she did need a babysitter after all.

She snapped the mirror shut and shoved it into her purse. Pulling her knees to her chest, she wrapped her arms around her legs and chewed her bottom lip. She didn't want to believe him. It sounded impossible, but the more she thought about last night, the more his explanation made sense.

That truck had hit her head-on, and she was still alive when it rolled over her like a speedbump, crushing her ribcage. She didn't imagine that. And Ethan... She didn't imagine what he'd done to her either. He'd bitten her neck, but it didn't hurt. After that, she could only recall waking up here. *Holy bloodsuckers.* She was a fucking vampire.

"This glamour of yours... Is that why I'm not scared of you? Why I don't remember anything after you bit me? Did you put me under some sort of spell?"

"The death sleep pulled you under shortly after I bit you, so you could complete the transformation. That's why you have no memory of arriving here. And it's natural for you to trust me. I sired you."

"Sired?"

"I turned you into a vampire."

"Ew. Okay, let's say that then. Saying you sired me makes it sound like you're my daddy or something, and that's a kink I could *never* get into." Ethan was way too hot to think of him as a father figure. Even with all the weirdness of discovering she'd been turned into a vampire—and this definitely took the cake for her weirdest experience yet —she still felt an underlying attraction to him. "I won't call you Daddy, no matter how much you beg."

The corner of his mouth twitched, but he still didn't smile.

She narrowed her eyes, vowing to make this man smile if it killed her. Could vampires die? "Are you always this serious?"

"This is a serious matter."

"Are all vampires this broody? Or is it just you?"

His eyes tightened. "We retain our personalities from our human lives."

"Oh, so this Edward Cullen act isn't an act? This is what you've always been like?"

He closed his eyes and went utterly still, so still, she wondered if he'd turned to stone. Could vampires do that? She had so many questions.

"Can you teach me to turn into a bat?"

He opened his eyes, and his jaw ticked again like he was annoyed. "No." What on Earth did he have to be annoyed about?

"Why did you save me?"

His eyes softened, a look of regret drawing down his brow. "I thought you were…" He clamped his mouth shut and shook his head. "You would have died. The sun has set. Let's get out of the attic."

"Thank God." Her throat closed up, and she fell into another coughing fit. "Why. Do. I. Keep. Coughing?" she asked between breaths.

Ethan squatted by the door, remaining silent until she finished nearly dying again. "I thought you'd have figured that out by now."

"Figured what out?"

He shook his head like he was disappointed. "Hundreds of years ago, after an unfortunate event involving an entire choir, the church smote our kind. We can't speak the name of a certain religious icon or his son without…" He gestured toward her. "Without *that* happening."

"You could have told me that after my first incident."

"I hoped you'd learn it on your own." He opened the attic door, and Jane shielded her eyes. No light sliced through the darkness this time.

"Is there anything else I need to know?" She followed him down a ladder into a narrow hallway.

"Plenty. You also can't go inside a church, and holy water burns." He led her into a small living room with a dark blue sofa and matching recliner. A television sat atop an oak entertainment center, and beige drapes covered the windows.

So not what she'd expected for a vampire's house. Where was his coffin, and shouldn't the upholstery be red velvet? "No holy stuff. Got it. What else?"

He stopped in front of the door and turned toward her. "You'll need to feed. We have to visit the Magistrate to get your permit, and then I'll teach you everything you need to know."

"Feed?" Her stomach sank. The shock of the situation had messed with her brain, and she hadn't stopped to consider what being a vampire actually meant. What she'd have to consume.

"You need blood to survive, but it's illegal to bite without a license." He opened the door, gesturing for her to exit. "Once you have your permit, I can teach you how to feed. Let's go."

The mere thought of biting a person…of drinking blood…had her head spinning. She swallowed the sour taste in her mouth, cringing as the cactus needles dug into her throat, and straightened her spine. She'd let him teach her how to glamour and do all the fun vampire shit, but there was no way in hell she'd be drinking blood.

CHAPTER FIVE

E than sent out one more mental distress signal to his sire and opened the front door. Unfortunately—though not unexpectedly—Gaston was nowhere to be found. He stepped onto the porch, closing his eyes and willing the sound of Jane's obnoxious voice to stop grating in his ears.

What had he done?

"Be a doll and get me a glass of water before we go, okay? I feel like I've swallowed a desert." Jane stood in the doorway, resting a hand against the jamb. Her dark hair hung in tangled knots, and smeared makeup marred her otherwise perfect complexion. Even in bloodied, torn clothes, the infuriating woman was stunningly beautiful.

Unfortunately, her superficial beauty didn't make it beneath her skin. He tilted his head, staring at her neck as she droned on about how thirsty she was. Actually, there was one beautiful thing beneath her skin. Her blood was as sweet as maraschino cherries. He'd never tasted anything like it. Beautiful on the outside, with sweet blood, but the positive traits ended there.

"Water won't quench your thirst." Her first taste of blood should be straight from the source, but he couldn't stand another minute of her whining. He stomped past her into the kitchen and took a glass from the cabinet, setting it on the countertop.

"You're right," she said. "A beer would be better. Or, hell, after what I've been through, I'll take a shot of whiskey."

He took a jug of O positive from the fridge. "You're a vampire, Jane. Only one thing will ease the burn in your throat."

"Whoa, Eddie." She held up her hands. "Is that blood?"

"Of course. What else would it be?"

She shook her head. "Don't pour it." She backed up until her butt met the counter. "Seriously, I just want water."

Without saying a word, he returned the jug to the fridge and filled the glass with tap water. If she wouldn't take his word for it, he'd let her learn the hard way. "Here you go, princess."

She snatched the glass from his hand. "Don't call me that."

"Don't call me Eddie."

"If you didn't act like such a brooding, teenage-romance vampire, I wouldn't."

"If you didn't act like such a stubborn, spoiled brat, neither would I."

Her mouth dropped open. "Jane Anderson is not spoiled."

"Riiight…" A tingle in the back of his mind alerted him to Gaston's approach. "Drink up. We've got company."

She chugged the water and slammed the glass on the counter before wiping her mouth with the back of her hand. "See? All better now. I just needed a drink."

"Uh huh." He stalked out the front door and descended the porch steps.

Gaston approached from above—in bat form, no less—his wings flapping wildly as he tilted from side to side, spiraling down before transforming into his human form. He stumbled as he hit the ground and caught himself on the porch railing.

Ethan shook his head. The sun hadn't been down a half-hour, and his sire was already lit.

Jane parked her hands on her hips and gaped. "Eddie, you fucking liar. You said I couldn't turn into a bat."

He groaned, giving Gaston the stink eye. His mentor had only done that to show off. "I said I couldn't teach you to turn into a bat. Gaston can shapeshift; I can't."

Sweeping the tails of his black duster behind him, Gaston stepped in front of Ethan and bowed at Jane. "How nice to finally see you conscious, Miss Jane. I'm sure Ethan has told you all about me."

She arched a brow, raking her gaze up and down his form. "Who are you?"

"I'm Gaston, Ethan's sire, of course." He went to lean a hand against the railing, but he missed by half a foot and stumbled into her.

Clutching his shoulders, she righted him and stepped back, looking at Ethan. "Is he drunk?"

Ethan lifted his shoulders, giving a slight nod. There weren't enough excuses in the world to make for Gaston. "He has a thing for Irish whiskey."

"It's rum tonight, my friend. A bachelorette party was drinking hurricanes."

Jane rolled her eyes. "Fantastic. It's just my luck to get turned into a vampire by an Edward Cullen wannabe who has Captain Jack Sparrow as his mentor."

Gaston held up a finger. "I resemble that remark."

"I think you mean 'resent,'" Ethan said.

Gaston smirked. "Do I?"

"When can I meet some real vampires?" She crossed her arms. "If I have to be a creature of the night, I want to learn all the tricks. Glamour, mind control, turning into a *bat*." She gave Ethan a pointed look.

"Shape-shifting magic can only be acquired by drinking copious amounts of were-blood," Gaston said. "Unfortunately, we've had a truce with the shifters for one hundred and fifty years, so I'm afraid that ability is out of reach for newly-turned vampires."

"Just…give me a minute. Gaston, can I talk to you privately?" He walked his sire out of Jane's earshot, though at this point, it wouldn't matter if she heard what he had to say. "I screwed up, man. You were right."

Gaston grinned. "What was I right about, old friend?"

"She's not Vanessa." Not even close, and the longer he looked at her, the less and less she resembled the memory of his fiancée. Hell, he couldn't even picture Vanessa's face at the moment, but he was positive she looked nothing like Jane.

"No? Are you sure? I remember Vanessa having long brown hair." Amusement danced in his ice-blue eyes.

Ethan gritted his teeth. "I'm positive." Vanessa was quiet, timid, mild-mannered. "She hasn't *shut* up since she *woke* up. What am I going to do? She talks about herself in the third person."

A deep laugh rumbled in Gaston's chest. "You're going

to take care of her like I took care of you. Train her. Make her the best vampire you can, then…and only then…you will set her free."

His breath came out in a hiss. "Can't you take her on? You're a fabulous sire. The best there is. She'd do much better having you train her."

Gaston clapped his shoulder. "Flattery will get you nowhere in this case, my friend. You made her; she is yours." He walked back toward the house, and Ethan followed. "Besides, she still bears your mark. No one else can touch her."

Jane had been sitting on the porch steps, but she shot to her feet. "His mark? What are you talking about?"

"She doesn't know?" Gaston looked far too amused. "He marked you, my dear. Did you not wonder why you haven't been the slightest bit afraid of a vampire? He claimed you as his own."

"Nobody *claims* Jane Anderson. I'm my own person, so you'd best remove that mark before you have to remove my boot from your ass." She shook her finger in Ethan's face.

He gladly would if he knew what to do, but he wasn't about to admit to this insolent woman that he had no clue how to remove it. He'd have to get Gaston to teach him in private. "When a vampire drinks from a human, he puts a temporary mark on them to let other vampires know they're low on blood. It's our system for keeping humans safe. We aren't allowed to drain anyone."

She pursed her lips, and for half a second, she almost looked disappointed. "That's all I was to you? A snack?"

For another half-second, he felt a twinge of guilt for hurting her feelings. "I didn't drink from you until I had to save your life. I marked you the night before so no one else would either, but the Magistrate doesn't need to know that."

She flinched as if she were slapped. "You didn't *want* to drink from me, but you also didn't want anyone else to? I don't understand."

He didn't understand why he felt the need to explain himself to her. Why—though her attitude drove him batshit crazy—he wanted to make her happy. It must have been the mating mark. As soon as he figured out how to remove it, these conflicting emotions would dissipate and his attraction to the woman would finally cease. "You were wasted, Jane. If I'd drunk from you, I'd have been wasted too, and someone needed to see you home safely."

A smug smile curved her lips. "Oh, Edward, you do care."

No, no, he didn't. These emotions weren't real. "The constables are out in full force lately. Let's get you registered so no one gets the stake."

"Neither of you can be in the Magistrate's presence looking like criminals." Gaston reached inside his jacket. "You both need a shower and a change of clothes before we go. Jane, dear, I took the liberty of stopping by your lovely house on my way. I think this crimson chenille sweater will suit your vampire-pale skin nicely, along with a pair of dark jeans."

He handed her the clothes. "Oh, I almost forgot the best part." He reached into his jacket again and pulled out a matching set of lingerie. The bra was black satin trimmed in lace, and the panties, what existed of them, were sheer with black lace around the waistband.

Ethan's throat thickened, his dick hardening as an image of what she'd look like wearing the lingerie—and nothing else—flashed in his mind. His fingers twitched as he imagined peeling the fabric from her body, a smile lighting on her lips as he trailed his tongue over her soft skin.

Jane snatched the clothing from Gaston's hand, her gaze locking with Ethan's for a moment before she looked away. "I was saving these for a special occasion. I suppose becoming a registered vampire will have to be good enough."

Gaston steepled his fingers, grinning like a fool. "Perhaps you can model them for us later."

"Fat chance. Where's the shower?"

"Down the hall. Second door on the left." He stared at her curvy backside as she sashayed into the house and disappeared around the corner. "She didn't have any more modest underwear?"

Gaston chuckled. "Mildly so, but I'm afraid our dear Jane is quite the firecracker. I think she's going to be good for you."

How in hell could she be good for him? They'd done nothing but bicker since she woke up. Then again, he hadn't *felt* this much in as long as he could remember. He leaned against the porch railing, trying to recall what exactly it was about Jane that had drawn him to her, made him think she was the woman he loved. He came up with nothing.

Yet, there was *something*.

"Well, well." Constable Watson appeared from around the corner, his trench coat flapping behind him as he strode up the sidewalk. "What kind of trouble are we getting into tonight, gentlemen?"

Ethan straightened his spine. "None at all, Constable."

Watson narrowed his eyes, glancing at the open front door. "Hmm."

"This one wouldn't know trouble if it bit his ass and drained him dry." Gaston stood between Watson and the entrance. "What kind are you looking for?"

"Anything, really." Watson glanced at his nails and buffed them on his lapel. "You've the highest concentration of supernatural beings on the continent in this city alone, yet I'm regretful to say I haven't found nearly as much mayhem as I'd hoped."

"Our Magistrate runs this city like a well-oiled machine," Ethan said. "What were you hoping to find?"

Watson shrugged. "Chaos. Disorder. Signs of a much-needed change in command. When this position with the SWO opened, I jumped at the chance to audit New Orleans. Alas, you're all too good at following the rules."

"All right, Eddie. Your turn." Jane strutted onto the porch, stepping around Gaston and crossing her arms, cocking her hip out as she gave Watson a once-over. "Nice hat."

Gaston was right about the red sweater flattering Jane's skin tone. It also hugged her curves, dipping just low enough to reveal a bit of cleavage and making Ethan's mouth water. Her damp hair hung past her shoulders, and her makeup-free skin had an ethereal glow.

Watson pulled his cell phone from his pocket. "May I see your license and registration, madam?"

"Madam?" Jane dropped her arms to her sides. "Do I look eighty to you?"

"She's not registered yet." Ethan positioned himself between the constable and Jane, but she stepped aside, refusing his protection.

A devilish smile curved Watson's lips. "Oh, dear. The

grace period has ended, I'm afraid. Perhaps tonight won't be as uneventful as I first thought." He pocketed his phone and rubbed his hands together. "It's been a while since I've gotten to stake anyone."

Ethan grabbed Jane's arm, shoving her behind his body and sandwiching her between him and Gaston. "You're not touching her. She's newly-turned, and we're on our way to see the Magistrate now."

"Laws are laws, and she should be registered. I'm sure you understand." Watson cracked his knuckles.

No way in the seven levels of hell was this asshole laying a finger on Jane. "She just woke up dead an hour ago. Fledglings have until the end of their first night to register."

"That is the law, an SWO law, I might add," Gaston said over Jane's shoulder. "Shall I make a call to the Magistrate and sort this out? I've known him since he was a fledgling himself."

Watson glowered, stepping back as he clasped his hands behind his back. "I'll be watching you. One mistake, and you'll be mine." He turned, jerking his coat so it waved like a cape, before disappearing around the corner.

"Now's there's a stereotypical vampire." Jane laughed, but it didn't mask the tremble in her voice. She slipped from between him and Gaston, reaching across her body to rub one arm. "Did he really want to stake me?"

"I wouldn't have let him." Ethan gripped her bicep softly, and her breath caught as he held her gaze.

She swallowed hard, cringing, though he wasn't sure if it was from the dryness in her throat or the threat to her life. "Thank you. You might be as sullen as a teenage guitar player, but you're a good man."

If she only knew.

Jane stood in the foyer of the vampire headquarters, trying to ignore the sensation of her underwear riding up her ass. That particular set of lingerie wasn't meant to be worn longer than a few minutes and never outside the bedroom. She ran her fingers through her damp hair, tousling it a bit to give it some lift. Even with all that dark, wavy, sexy hair, Mr. Broody Vampire didn't own a hairdryer. She looked in an antique mirror hanging on the wall of the nineteenth-century mansion's foyer and marveled at her complexion. She was a few shades paler than she'd been before, but otherwise, her skin was perfect. Once she got ahold of some eyeliner and mascara, she'd be smokin' hot.

This vampire gig was turning out to be a blessing. She had super strength, which she'd figured out when she pushed Ethan earlier, and when Gaston had fallen and she'd picked him up like he was light as a cotton ball. She was gorgeous, immortal, and the only things that could kill her were stakes to the heart, beheading, and sunlight, which, to be honest, already killed a lot of people anyway. *Skin cancer's a bitch.*

The only drawback to her condition was the blood-drinking issue, but Jane was resourceful. She'd figure out a way to find sustenance. That water hadn't quenched her thirst at all, but she'd never tell Ethan that. Maybe she could order her steaks rare. That might work.

She'd have to watch all her friends and family die eventually, but death was inevitable. She'd miss Sophie the most. "Oh, shit. Sophie. She must be worried sick about me." She sank onto the little couch next to Ethan.

"I used your phone to text her. She knows you're with me." He stared straight forward, his face unreadable. Only his fists clenched in his lap gave away his emotions, and she still couldn't tell if he was angry or nervous. And what was he angry or nervous about? That British twit who wanted to stake her an hour after she woke up or the whole situation of having to register a new vampire?

Her stomach fluttered again when she thought about the way he'd jumped in front of her, protecting her as if he cared.

"What did you tell her?" She pulled her phone from her purse and swiped open the messaging app. Her eyes widened as she read the exchange:

Ethan (pretending to be Jane): *Hey. I ran into that hot guy who took us home last night. I'm going to spend the night with him.*

Sophie: *You go, girl. I can't wait to hear all about him.*

She cast Ethan a sideways glance. "'That hot guy?' Seriously?"

He shrugged. "I was trying to be authentic."

She snorted. The man had nerve—and possible mind-reading abilities. She continued reading their texts.

Sophie (twelve hours later): *Wow, he must have ridden you hard and put you up sopping wet. What time are you coming back?*

Ethan: *Actually, I'm going to spend the day with him. He's amazing.*

Sophie: *K. Stay safe and use protection.*

She dropped the phone into her purse. "'Amazing?' You're full of yourself, aren't you?"

"Would she believe you'd spend the day with me if I were anything less?"

Jane narrowed her eyes. "I have to see her tonight. She

definitely won't believe I'd ditch her two nights in a row. What's taking Gaston so long, anyway? He disappeared fifteen minutes ago to 'introduce' us to the Magistrate."

Ethan closed his eyes. "Vampire politics are complicated."

Jane rolled hers. "I know more about politics than you can shake your dick at."

"That's not how the saying goes."

"My dad's the governor of Texas."

He glanced at her. "That explains a lot."

"What's that supposed to mean?"

His nostrils flared as he let out a slow breath. "You expect others to do everything for you. With a father in a position of high authority, now I understand why."

"Because you think I'm spoiled." Which she *so* wasn't. She worked her ass off to earn the respect of the men in her family, and for what? Her own father still thought she needed a babysitter.

"I won't fault you for your upbringing, but I won't enable you either."

"Enable me? Oh my Go—olly gosh jeez." She crossed her arms. "See, I can learn."

His brow lifted, and the corners of his mouth twitched. Did the man ever smile? Why did she want him to so badly?

"You need to lighten up," she said. "If I'm going to be part of your clan, you'll have to learn to have fun."

"It's a coven, not a clan."

"I thought witches had covens."

He closed his eyes for another long blink. "They do. Vampires do too."

"And werewolves?"

"Packs, of course."

She chewed her bottom lip, taking in her surroundings. A thick burgundy rug covered most of the hardwood floor, and dark wood furniture gave the room a period vibe. "Are there any werewolves in New Orleans?"

"Plenty."

"Are they our natural-born enemies?"

His nostrils flared again. "That's a myth."

"Am I annoying you?"

"Very much."

Was he serious? *She* was annoying *him*? "You're the one who turned *me* into a vampire. And you never told me why you did it. Everyone dies. Why did you choose to save me?"

"Jane." He turned toward her, taking her shoulders in his hands.

His grip was firm, yet somehow gentle at the same time, and his touch set off a chemical reaction inside her body. She shouldn't have been attracted to him. He had all the personality of a wet tissue, but there she was, staring into his emerald eyes while he smoldered back at her, warmth blooming in her nether region, threatening to soak her lace panties.

His gaze flicked to her mouth for half a second before he released her. "You haven't stopped talking since you woke up."

She brushed her hair from her forehead, composing herself. "What do you expect? I'm suddenly not human anymore, and I have questions."

"I know you do, but I didn't plan this. I... In a city that never sleeps, I value silence. I've been alone for the past twenty-five years, and I'm not used to..." He closed his eyes and took a deep breath. "Give me five minutes of peace. Please. Can you keep your mouth shut for five minutes so I can get my thoughts together?"

She narrowed her eyes, chewing the inside of her cheek. If he wanted silence, she'd give him silence...and a cold shoulder to go with it.

Rising to her feet, she stepped toward a baby grand piano sitting in the back corner of the room. She lightly ran her fingers across the cool ivory keys, stopping at middle C and giving it a tap. The note rang out, filling the room with music.

"I asked for silence," Ethan grumbled.

She raised her hands. "Okay, okay." Her boots thudded on the hardwood floor as she strolled toward the window. Behind the curtain rod, a mechanical device was mounted to the frame. She flipped the red switch on the wall next to it—because c'mon, a red switch? How could she not flip it?—and the device hummed to life, a thick black shade sliding down to cover the window.

"Jane!" Ethan didn't move from his spot on the couch, but his tone was sharp enough to slice skin.

"Sorry. Couldn't help myself." She flipped the switch in the opposite direction, and the shade rolled back up. "How come you don't have something like this at your house? Wouldn't you rather sleep in your bedroom than up in the dusty old attic?"

"They're too expensive."

"Vampires need money?"

"How else would we buy things?"

She plopped onto the couch next to him. It had been five minutes, hadn't it? Close enough. "What's it like having Captain Jack Sparrow as your mentor? Is he always so...drunk?"

"Gaston is a good sire and a good friend. He's been

around more than three hundred years, so I can only imagine the things he's seen. What he's been through." He unclenched his fists and laid his palms on his thighs. "He gets this way during Mardi Gras. With so many drunk humans in the Quarter, he can't seem to help himself."

"Is that it? Or did something happen to him during a past Mardi Gras, and he's trying to numb the pain?"

Ethan looked at her as if he'd never considered the idea. "I don't know. He doesn't talk about his past much, unless it's to recount a fight. Nobody fights like Gaston."

Jane giggled. "What about cheap shots? I bet nobody takes those like Gaston either."

"He does what he has to do."

"Is he good at expectorating? *Especially* good?" She was cracking herself up.

He blinked. "What does that have to do with anything?"

"Oh, come on. Haven't you seen *Beauty and the Beast*? Gaston is the bad guy, and he has a fantastic song."

"No."

"How old are you?"

"I've been dead for twenty-five years."

She narrowed her eyes, studying him. "You look like you're in your early twenties, which means you've been around for about forty-eight years or so. Am I right?"

"He nodded."

"I know what your problem is. You're a Gen Xer"

His brow arched. "And your point is?"

"You don't give a shit about anything."

"And you're an entitled Millennial who thinks the world owes her everything."

She crossed her arms. "You don't know anything about me."

"I know enough."

The door Gaston had disappeared through finally opened, and he stepped into the room, grinning as it closed behind him. "Come, children. The Magistrate awaits."

CHAPTER SIX

Jane strutted toward the door, stopping in front of it as Gaston whispered something to Ethan, who grimaced and whispered something back through clenched teeth. These boys needed a lesson in subtlety… and manners.

Ethan stepped behind her. "What are you waiting for? Let's get this over with."

"I'm waiting for someone to open the door for me."

"You're capable of opening it yourself."

She gaped, waiting for him to take the hint and open the damn thing like a gentleman, but he just stood there staring at her like she was out of her mind for expecting chivalry. "Fine." She yanked on the knob and stomped into the hallway, but Ethan caught her by the arm, holding her back as Gaston passed.

"There's an order to things here. The senior vampire enters first. Do you remember everything we taught you on the way over?"

She tugged from his grasp and straightened her sweater. Why the hell did he make her open the door if

Gaston had to go in before her anyway? "Of course. I'm not an idiot."

He walked next to her toward a set of double doors. "They'll ask us some questions, and then you'll recite the rules you learned. You can answer everything honestly, but if you want us to make it out alive, I did not mark you until *after* I drank from you. Got it?"

"You want me to lie under oath?" She pressed a hand to her chest, feigning shock. Her dad was a politician. She learned to lie from the best.

"It's against the law to mark someone unless you've drunk from them. I could get the stake for it." His eyes were even more serious than normal.

No way in hell would she let some vampire Council kill Ethan for trying to protect her. He may have been as fun as a pap smear, but the man did save her life. Twice. She patted his cheek. "Don't worry, darlin'. I won't tell a soul." She owed him that much.

Gaston threw open the doors and strode into the room.

"Stay two steps behind me," Ethan whispered as he crossed the threshold.

She was about to protest that Jane Anderson stayed behind no man, but the sight of the Council froze her to the spot.

Four men in black robes sat atop a raised platform in gold and gem-encrusted thrones. Jane squinted, trying to determine the types of jewels and whether or not they were real. If they were, this room alone would be worth a fortune.

The men looked old as the gods themselves, with shoulder-length, scraggly hair and skin so paper-thin, she could have torn it with a fingernail—and Jane always got the "squoval" when she had a manicure. Stilettos belonged on the feet, not the hands.

"I thought vampires didn't age."

"These guys don't get out much. With little interaction in the modern world, they've lost touch with most of their human traits." Ethan grabbed her hand, tugging her into the room, and his touch sent another jolt through her body. They stopped in the middle of the room, and he released her, while Gaston joined a group of vampires along the wall.

Gas lamps enclosed in glass cases provided the only light in the room, but Jane could see just fine—another plus to this vampire business. The windows lining the right side of the room were all equipped with the same light-blocking mechanism as the sitting-room window, and the long, rectangular shape of the room made it look like it might have been a grand ballroom back in the day.

Upon closer inspection, the vampire Council didn't seem quite so elderly. More like scary...and incredibly bored. "Holy shit, Edward. You didn't tell me we were coming to meet the Volturi."

"Shh..."

A door opened behind the dais, and a man who could only be the Magistrate drifted in. He wore the same black robes as the Council members, and his movements were so fluid, he seemed to float above the floor. His long, dark hair was woven into dreads, making him look like Idris Elba in that *Thor* movie, but he had a menacing glint in his eyes and crackling power in his aura that screamed authority. With his strong jaw and piercing hazel eyes, he was sexy as all get-out, but not someone Jane wanted to piss off.

Idris sank into the center throne, and Jane waved. "Hey, guys. Nice to meet you."

Every single one of those suckers leaned toward her, hissing—literally hissing—as they bared their fangs. She parked her hands on her hips and turned to Ethan. "Is this for real? Are they hissing?"

His nostrils flared for the umpteenth time tonight as his hands curled into fists. "You don't address the Council without permission to speak."

"You could have told me that beforehand. Nobody hisses at Ja—"

Ethan bared his fangs and hissed at her too.

Her mouth fell open. "Oh. My. Go— goat cheese pizza. Not you too." She ran her tongue along her teeth. No fangs, but she refused to be out-hissed. She bared her blunt teeth and did her best angry cat impression. Then she turned to the Council and hissed at them for good measure. *Jesus Christ.* Hey, at least she could still swear in her head. She was stuck in the middle of a *What We Do in the Shadows* episode.

Ethan clapped his hand over her mouth and wrapped his other arm around her from behind. "Apologies, Magistrate. She's freshly turned and ornery as hell. I don't quite have her under control yet."

Control? Who did he think he was? She tried to protest, but he kept his hand pressed tightly against her mouth.

The Magistrate nodded. "You will apprise her of the laws and exert your control as her sire."

"Yes, sir."

The moment he released her, she whirled to face him. "Let's get one thing straight, Eddie. You don't control me. No one does. And why are there no women on this Council? Is this a patriarchy? Because I'm all about busting glass ceilings."

Ethan growled low in his throat. "Permission to stake her, Your Honor?"

She gasped. "You wouldn't dare."

"Try me."

"Enough." The Magistrate had an *I don't get paid enough for this shit* look on his face, so Jane clamped her mouth shut. She could totally feel for the guy. Her own bullshit meter didn't go very high either. "You will recite the rules to receive your permit."

Jane rattled off all the crap Ethan wanted her to memorize on their way over: She had to stay with her sire —*ew*, that word still didn't sit right with her—at all times until she was licensed; she wasn't allowed to bite anyone— not that she ever would…EVER—until she'd been properly trained, and a bunch of other nonsense about not leaving bite marks and only using her glamour responsibly.

This Council took all the fun out of being an undead creature of the night.

Ethan let out what sounded like a breath of relief when she was done…as if he'd actually been worried she'd fail the test. *Please*, Jane had never failed a test in her life. Not one she studied for, anyway.

When she was done, the Magistrate steepled his fingers and rested his elbows on the arms of his jewel-encrusted throne. "Very good. You will be tested for your biting license in three weeks." He glanced at the man next to him. "Put her on the schedule." He turned to address Ethan. "How did this pairing come about, and why has the mating mark not been reciprocated?"

Jane blinked. "Mating mark?"

Gaston snickered from his spot on the sidelines, and Ethan hung his head. "It was an accident, Your Honor." Ethan lifted his gaze to Jane's and looked away, ashamed.

"Umm…" Jane's mouth opened and closed a few times before she could form words, which was probably a good thing. She didn't want to engage in another hissing match. "Permission to speak?"

The Magistrate nodded.

She turned to Ethan. "What the hell is a mating mark? You said you marked me as a meal."

"She's unaware you've claimed her as your mate?" The Magistrate leaned forward, the boredom in his eyes morphing into curiosity. "Please explain."

Ethan cast Gaston a *help me out here* glance, but his sire just laughed, shaking his head. He looked at Jane again before focusing on the Magistrate. "I…thought she was someone else when I turned her. I made a mistake."

Jane tilted her head. "Which was the mistake? Turning me into a vampire or marking me as your mate?"

He pursed his lips, hesitating to answer. "Both."

"Well, shit." Her knees suddenly weak, she plopped onto the floor, sitting cross-legged and holding her head in her hands. It shouldn't matter. She didn't want to be his mate, and the vampire thing…what was done was done, but…

The fact that not only did he not want her, but he didn't even want her to be a vampire, was like a knife—no, like a stake—to her heart. She shouldn't have cared, and maybe it was the shock of this whole situation wearing off and her real emotions breaking through, but pressure mounted in the back of her eyes, and a sob attempted to bubble up her throat. Thankfully, she was so parched, the sob didn't make it past her chest.

She flopped onto her back dramatically. "Go ahead and stake me. You heard the man; I'm a mistake. He doesn't want me."

"Come now, Jane. Let's not be dramatic." Gaston lifted her to her feet.

"You're one to talk, Captain Jack."

He laughed and pinched her cheek. "I like you." He motioned Ethan over and wrapped an arm around both of them. "It's true he thought you were someone else, but I distinctly remember him saying he didn't care if you weren't her right before he turned you."

She stared at Ethan until he met her gaze. "Is that true?"

He held eye contact. "Yes."

"So you don't regret turning me into a vampire?"

"Well…" he began, but he jumped when Gaston pinched him. "Honestly? No, I don't regret it. I find you…interesting."

"Interesting? Like a science experiment?"

"Intriguing."

She smiled, and the imaginary stake slipped from her chest. "I'll take intriguing."

"You wear it well," Ethan said.

The Magistrate cleared his throat. "Now that your domestic dispute has been settled, the mark must either be removed or reciprocated."

"Removed, please." Jane stepped out of Gaston's embrace. "I hardly know him."

"I'd love to remove it." Ethan's hands curled into fists. "But I don't even know how I put it on you. It just happened."

"Interesting." The Magistrate steepled his fingers again, drumming them together like he was amused. "Subconsciously applied marks are rare. Perhaps we should require it stays."

"No, please." Ethan pressed his palms together. "It was my mistake. I'll take responsibility, but please don't punish her. She deserves a choice."

Her eyebrows shot up. *Wow.* Mr. Sexy Brooding Vampire had a heart.

"Very well." The Magistrate rose to his feet and looked at Gaston. "I assume you are coherent enough to instruct him in mark removal?"

"Of course, Your Honor." Gaston bowed as the Council filed out of the room, and then he whispered something in Ethan's ear.

Ethan nodded and placed his hands on either side of Jane's head. Her skin tingled, and electricity shot through her core, gathering below her navel. His eyes turned stormy, like a sea at night, and her knees wobbled. This guy was sex on a stick.

Something seemed to snap inside her; the cord that had been tugging her toward him was severed, leaving a small, hollow space in her heart. She rubbed at the spot where she felt the discomfort, and he dropped his arms to his sides, stepping back and sweeping his gaze over her.

"It's done." Something she wanted to call regret flashed briefly in his eyes.

She wanted to call it regret because that was the only name she could find for her own emotions at the moment. Why on Earth would she feel that way? Being tied down to a man was the last thing she wanted, yet she already missed the connection to him. *You're going cuckoo, Jane. Woman up.*

"Good job, my friend." Gaston patted him on the

back. "Now, any emotions you felt for each other that were fabricated by the mark will cease."

"Thank the l—lady next door. Every time he touched me, I wanted to rip his clothes off. That'll go away now?"

Surprise widened Ethan's eyes, and a bit of a blush reddened his cheeks. How cute. Wait a minute. She wasn't supposed to be feeling attraction to him anymore.

Gaston chuckled. "Time will tell."

"Do you have a driver's license?" Ethan asked. "I need to fill out the paperwork to register you."

"I'm capable of filling it out myself."

He shook his head. "It has to be completed by the sire."

"Ew." She wrinkled her nose.

He rolled his eyes. "By the person who turned you."

"Here. It's from Texas, but it'll have to do." She tugged the license from her pocket, handing it to him, and he shuffled into the next room.

"So." She turned to Gaston. "Who did he think I was when he turned me?"

Gaston smiled sadly and shook his head. "The poor sap thought you were his dead fiancée reincarnated. I told him you were your own woman, but he wanted you to be her so badly."

Poor guy. "No wonder he's disappointed. What happened to her?"

"That's his story to tell, I'm afraid." He leaned in closer. "Honestly, I don't remember all the details. He can be quite the…what's the phrase? Drama queen."

Jane giggled and then bit her lip as she caught a glimpse of Ethan through the doorway. He leaned over a desk, filling out a form, and she swept her gaze to his backside, admiring the way his jeans hugged his muscular thighs.

"You still find yourself attracted to him, even without the mark?"

He had a broad back and strong shoulders—and that ass…scrumptious. "He is easy on the eyes. Are these feelings going to wear off since the mark is gone?"

Gaston grinned. "Time will tell."

"You already said that."

"Miss Jane, I believe you're going to be good for our friend Ethan."

She tore her gaze away from his magnificent derriere. "Do you now?"

"He's had a stake wedge up his ass since I turned him. Hopefully, you can remove it."

Jane laughed. "I'll make it my mission."

CHAPTER SEVEN

"Good luck, my friend." Gaston slapped Ethan on the back and grinned. He even had the nerve to laugh, the bastard. "I'm just a thought away if you need me." He spun on his heel and disappeared into the crowd.

Jane strutted next to Ethan, matching his pace as he strode up Royal Street. "Oh, that's cute." She paused to look at a red vintage-style dress, reminiscent of the 1950s, in a shop window. "Too bad these stores aren't open after dark. I'll have to see if I can order this online."

He started to complain that they needed to be on their way, but she was registered and had her biting permit. Other than teaching her how to feed, they had no pressing plans. He'd just damned her to a life of darkness; he could give her a moment to look at a pretty dress. Hell, if he could afford it, he'd buy the damn thing. She'd look amazing in it.

His face pinched at the thought. He'd figured—he'd hoped—that as soon as the mating mark was removed, his attraction to her would cease. But other than the little hollow space in his chest, he didn't feel any differently about the confounding woman.

She was loud, entitled, and extremely annoying, yet every time she smiled, his sluggish heart beat a little bit faster. And now that he knew what she was wearing beneath her form-fitting sweater and jeans, he couldn't get the image out of his mind. She wasn't the only one who felt the desire to tear off clothing every time they touched.

There was a simple solution for that. He just wouldn't touch her. He hadn't felt attraction to anyone since Vanessa died. No need to change things now.

"Hey. You okay?" She placed her hand on his arm, sending a jolt to his heart and yanking him out of the daydream he'd lost himself in.

"Yeah. Fine." He rubbed the spot where she'd touched him, trying to erase the images flashing through his mind of her rubbing *another* spot...a spot that hadn't been touched in years. He stepped back, out of arm's reach.

"What did Gaston mean by just a thought away? Can y'all put thoughts into each other's heads?"

He shoved his hands into his pockets. "We can."

Her dark eyes sparkled. "Can you teach me to do that? Can you do it to anyone?"

"I will eventually, and you can, but it takes time and intense practice to communicate with anyone other than your sir— the person who turned you." She was right. Calling him her sire did sound wrong. He wasn't into the daddy fetish either.

She smiled. "Now is as good a time as any."

"Your constant talking already grates in my ears. I don't need you inside my mind too."

"Whoa." She clutched her head. "You don't have to be

so rude." Her smile returned. "I've got to learn how to do that."

"More importantly, you need to learn how to feed. Let's leave the Quarter and find dinner, shall we?"

Her nose crinkled. "Let's have dinner *in* the French Quarter."

"That's not a good idea for your first time. During Mardi Gras, most of the people are drunk, and the alcohol in their blood will affect you. I'd hate for you to end up like Gaston."

She pressed her lips together, a disgusted expression contorting her features. "Let's have *food* for dinner. We can still eat, right?"

"Well, yes, but it provides no sustenance, and you only have three weeks to learn the proper biting techniques to get your license."

"Why do we have to be licensed anyway?" She continued strolling along the sidewalk…and talking before he could answer her question. "We're at the top of the food chain; we should be able to do whatever we want."

"Our kind has an agreement with the human government." He walked next to her, but far enough away that she couldn't touch him casually. He had to get his reactions to her under control. "We follow a set of rules, and we coexist in peace."

She stopped and faced him, her eyes widening. "The human government knows vampires exist?"

"They know about all the supernatural beings. Part of the arrangement is for them to help keep our existence a secret."

Her mouth hung open. "So my dad knows vampires are real?"

"He most likely does, but I don't recommend you tell

him you are one until you're officially licensed." *Or at all.* Ethan had no idea how the Texas government felt about supes. Fear could drive people to madness.

"Unbelievable." She shook her head and chewed her bottom lip, looking thoughtful and awfully cute. "What happens if I miss the deadline? I've got plenty of money. I can pay a fine."

"Unlicensed vampires pay with their lives. The punishment is the stake."

"No one in their right mind would even think about staking the Governor's daughter." She waved a hand dismissively. "This is only my third night in the city. I have a super-long to-do list, and trying all the amazing food is a big part of it. Please? Sophie is meeting me at the rental house in two hours. That's plenty of time for us to have dinner and get to know each other."

"I don't know, Jane." A strange desire to make her happy tightened his chest, but restaurants in the French Quarter weren't cheap. He hadn't worked in weeks, and he barely had enough to pay the water bill this month.

"I may be a vampire, but I still have a job to do. My Instagram has been silent for more than twenty-four hours, and that's not a good thing in my line of work." She hooked an arm around his elbow. "C'mon. It'll be my treat. I can write it off as a business expense."

This close to her, he could smell his shampoo mixed with her own sweet scent, and damn it if it wasn't the most delicious aroma to entice his senses in ages. "Do you always get what you want?"

"Most of the time, yes."

He didn't have the energy to argue with her. Besides, it had been years since he'd had a bite of human food, and Jane still seemed healthy enough. Her body would finish processing her own human blood soon, and then she'd require a real vampire meal.

"Okay. But after you see Sophie, you need to start your lessons. I'll do the biting in the beginning, and you simply drink. There will be two puncture wounds from my fangs, directly in a vein, so you'll create suction with your lips around the wound. Hopefully your fangs will come in soon, and you can learn to do the biting yourself."

She pressed her lips into a hard line, giving her head a tiny shake. "There's got to be a way to sustain ourselves on human food."

"There isn't."

"How do you know? Have you tried?"

"We are *undead*. Our own blood has thickened to the point of sludge. Our hearts beat once every ten seconds, barely moving that sludge through our systems. We require the nutrients of fresh blood daily, or we will shrivel up and waste away."

Her eye twitched every time he said the word "blood." "Jeez Louise, Edward. Do you have to be so morbid?" She gestured across the street. "I heard that place is good. Let's grab a bite and talk about something less nauseating."

He followed her across the street and into Royal House Oyster Bar. A massive mirror hung behind a long, wood bar, and three men stood between, shucking fresh oysters and arranging them on platters for the patrons. Tables lined the walkway between the bar and the front windows before the restaurant opened up into an expansive dining area.

The hostess led them to a table near the kitchen, but Jane paused, batted her lashes, and touched the hostess on the elbow. "Would it be at all possible to get the table by the front window?" She slipped a folded bill into the woman's hand, and the hostess nodded, weaving her way toward the table Jane asked for.

Impressive. "I may not have to teach you any glamour at all. You seem to do fine without it." Ethan opened the menu and peered at her over the top.

She shrugged. "When I promise to be a good girl, Daddy lets me be seen in public with him. I've bumped elbows with plenty of people in power. I know how things are done."

"A good girl?"

She folded the menu on the table. "Two of my brothers are lawyers; one's a CPA, and the other is a doctor. You could say I'm a disappointment. In fact, you probably have said that in your mind at least once since you turned me."

Initially, yes, he did think that. But if he were honest, he'd have to admit he hadn't been this entertained in years. And for the first time in forever, he felt like his life had purpose. Even if it was simply to teach the woman to feed herself, he had something meaningful to do.

"My dad wanted me to go to law school too," she continued, "but I couldn't bring myself to work those hours. I got a degree in communications, and I blog about my adventures. Of course, now that I'm a vampire, I'll have to figure out what I'm going to do. Can we travel easily? Do we need to have coffins shipped like we're dead bodies, or can we fly like regular people?"

She droned on and on, only stopping her laundry list of questions to order her meal: a Taste of New Orleans with etouffée, gumbo, and jambalaya all on one plate.

"I'll have the roast beef po-boy." Ethan handed his menu to the waiter.

"Oh, that sounds good. I'll have one of those too. I'm

starving." She looked at him. "What's the best drink to ease the burning in my throat?"

He arched a brow. "I believe you know."

She nodded. "Beer. I'll take a tall Abita Amber too, please."

He shook his head. When Gaston first turned him, he'd been somewhat averse to drinking blood, but the thirst quickly overpowered his hesitation. She'd give in eventually.

Their food arrived, and Jane devoured everything on her plate, sucking down her beer like it could save her life. Ethan ate half of his po-boy and a few fries. The savory beef with gravy and bits of debris, little pieces of meat that simmered for hours in the bottom of the pan, were as delicious as he remembered. He'd have to take a moment to enjoy a human meal every now and then in the future.

Jane leaned back in her chair and patted her stomach. "That was the best food I've ever had in my life. It's weird because I'm full, but I'm still hungry." She rubbed her throat. "I guess thirsty is a better word for it. Parched."

"You'll remain that way until you feed."

She visibly shivered. "Just let me make a few notes about this place for my blog, and then we can go. Remind me to get my charger from Sophie too. My phone's almost dead." Her laugh turned into a snort. "Almost dead...like us!"

⁂

"Well, well. Look what the cat dragged in." Sophie crossed her arms, grinning, and leaned against the door jamb as Jane tugged Ethan up the front walk. "There are thousands, if not millions of people in the French Quarter right now, and you found *him* again." She gave him a once-over with an approving nod. "What are the odds?"

You have no idea. "Hey, girl." Jane dropped Ethan's hand and pulled Sophie into a tight hug. "I have *so* much to tell you."

"I want every delectable detail."

The only delectable thing so far was dinner tonight… oh, and the fact she'd never grow old. That was a tasty little morsel she couldn't wait to share. "Ethan, you remember Sophie?"

"She puked on my shoes. How could I forget?"

Sophie cringed. "Sorry about that. Come on in." She stepped to the side and motioned for them to enter. "And in case Jane hasn't said it yet, thank you for not murdering us that night."

"Someone had to see you home safely."

"Yeah, but you could have just as easily been the thing we needed to stay safe from, so…" She shut the door and paused, cocking her head at Jane. "You look different. I mean, besides the no-makeup look, which you are totally rocking. Did you get a new moisturizer?"

Jane grinned. "I look good, don't I?"

"Fabulous. What's your secret?"

"Ethan turned me into a vampire."

Sophie laughed. "Fine. Don't tell me."

Ethan sank into a chair and crossed his arms. He wasn't keen on Jane telling Sophie what happened, but she'd convinced him the only way to keep the secret was to tell her best friend. Besides, he still insisted Sophie was a witch, so what did it matter?

"It's true. Ethan, show her your fangs."

He shook his head, looking perturbed, as usual. "I don't perform on command."

Jane rolled her eyes. "How else is she going to believe me?"

"He doesn't have fangs, and neither do you." Sophie put her hands on her hips. "Are you making fun of me because my grandma was a witch?"

"I told you she smells like a witch," Ethan said.

"I do?" Sophie lifted her arm and sniffed her pit.

"Listen," Jane said, "I don't have fangs because they haven't come in yet, but he does. Please, Ethan? Show her?"

He pressed his lips into a hard line, and when he peeled them back, revealing his pearly white fangs, a little thrill shimmied through Jane's body. Who knew she'd find teeth sexy?

"No way. Are those real?" Sophie leaned in for a closer look, and Ethan clamped his mouth shut. She went through the same stages of denial that Jane did, only Sophie didn't have to be nearly burned alive by sunlight to convince her. Instead, she perched on the arm of the sofa and smiled smugly. "I told you vampires were real."

"And you were right."

"Do you feel okay?" Her eyes widened. "Do you have to kill people now?"

"No, there are laws and junk. Ethan's supposed to teach me all of it: magic, glamour, and the boring rules. I'll live forever, never age, and I have super strength and speed."

"But you have to drink blood to survive." Sophie gave her a *how the hell are you going to pull that off?* look, and Jane glared back. That was all it took for her friend to get the message that her aversion to blood hadn't been mentioned yet. Best friends were awesome like that.

"I'm going to figure out a way to sustain myself on

human food. Jambalaya, though incredibly delicious, doesn't cut it, so I'm thinking maybe rare steak."

Ethan rubbed his forehead. "We've been through this, Jane. You require blood, and you only have three weeks to get your license."

"License?" Sophie laughed. "You need a license to drink blood?"

Jane shrugged. "It's a biting license. If I'm not biting anyone, I don't see why I need one."

"Because it's the law." Ethan pleaded with his eyes. Why did he have to look so damn cute when he did that?

"What happens if you don't get your license?"

"She'll be staked," he said.

"They'll kill you for not getting your license? That seems harsh."

"It's a new law. The Supernatural World Order is cracking down on unlicensed biting, and we've got a British constable in town forcing us to comply. She needs to learn the proper biting techniques, or she won't be around much longer."

Sophie's eyes softened. "Is that true, Jane?"

Jane scoffed. "My dad is the Governor of Texas. They wouldn't dare lay a fang on me."

"That's true. I can't imagine they'd want that kind of publicity for the state. If the Texas Governor's daughter goes missing in Louisiana, that could cause all kinds of trouble." Sophie stood next to Jane. "The government knows about the vampires, right? I'm sure there's some kind of conspiracy going on to keep magic a secret from normal people. Like in *The Originals*. Remember that show?"

Jane nodded. "I do, and it's just like that, except the vampire Council would fit better in a B movie."

Sophie snickered. "I bet that's a hoot. I'd love to meet them."

Ethan leaned his head back on the chair and let out a long, slow, dramatically loud breath.

Sophie leaned closer and whispered, "Is he always so…"

"Grumpy? Serious? Boring? Ornery?"

"Well…is he?"

"All of the above. He thinks I talk too much." He opened one eye, and she blew him a kiss. If she didn't know any better, she'd have said the corner of his mouth twitched like he was fighting a smile. She might just yank that stake out of his ass yet. "I'm going to pack my bag, darlin'. I'll only be a minute."

"Sure thing, princess."

She pursed her lips, fighting her own smile, and grabbed Sophie's arm, leading her down the hallway to her bedroom. "I hate to leave you like this, but I have to stay with him. It's *the law,* and I'll fry in the sunlight, so…" She tugged her suitcase from beneath the bed and began tossing her things inside it.

"I can't believe my BFF is a vampire. I'm going to have to check out the local witch stores and see if I can get inside their circle." She ducked into the bathroom and returned with Jane's toiletry bag. "Have you met any were-wolves? That's what I really need. A big, burly man with lots of chest hair that I can run my fingers through, and we can howl at the moon together."

Jane laughed. "If I meet anyone who fits that description, I'll be sure to let you know."

"So…" Sophie crossed her arms and drummed her hot pink nails on her biceps. "You've given me details, but not the juicy ones. What's Mr. Uptight like in the sack? Is he an angel on the streets, a demon in the sheets, or what?"

She closed her suitcase and zipped it shut. "I wish I could answer that for you, but I have no idea."

Sophie's mouth dropped open. "You spent the night with the hottest man in New Orleans, and you didn't sleep with him?"

"I was nearly killed by a car, and then he turned me into a vampire. It wasn't exactly the most romantic of nights. Besides..." She lowered her gaze as her stomach soured. "For one thing, he doesn't like me very much, and for another... He thought I was his dead fiancée. That's why he turned me."

"Like reincarnated? Are you?"

"No, definitely not, but... Personality-wise, he's not my type at all. There's something about him though."

"He is hot. I'd do him."

"Girl, me too. He could just lie there dead to the world, as long his dick is hard and proportionate to the rest of him. With that body, I could have a blast on my own."

"You know I can hear you, right? Did I not mention vampires' above average hearing?"

Jane clutched her head. "Crap. He's listening. Come outside with me for a sec. I need a favor, and it's none of Edward Cullen's business." She yelled the last part just to grate on his nerves.

Sophie followed her out the back door and whispered, "That man swept you out of your Nikes before you realized they were untied. You really like him, don't you?"

"I don't know. Maybe. He did turn me into this fabulous creature." She gestured at herself. "The problem is, he's got us sleeping in his dusty old attic. I think he's poor and can't afford the light-blocking gadgets, which I know exist because I've seen them. So, I need you to go to the bank for me and take out some cash. I'm going to talk to his friend Gaston and see about having his place fixed up. It's the least I can do to show my appreciation."

"Janey's got a boyfriend," Sophie sang.

Jane shook her head. "I'd be dead now if it weren't for him."

"Actually, you kinda are."

CHAPTER EIGHT

"Oh. My. Goat cheese pizza. An ice cream shop!" Jane grabbed Ethan's sleeve and tugged him across the street. "I could use some mint chocolate chip therapy right now."

What she could have used was a pint of O positive, but his attempts to get her to feed over the past two weeks had been fruitless. She was becoming pale and weaker, sleeping fitfully during the days and sluggish to awaken at night. He'd heard of starvation being used as punishment for unruly vampires—before the Supernatural World Order decided the stake would be the cure for everything —but he'd never witnessed anyone starve themselves on purpose.

"Come on, slowpoke." She held the door open and motioned for him to enter.

Reaching above her head, he grasped the edge of the door. "After you, princess."

Her smile warmed his cold heart, which was why he'd given in to some of her whims, opening doors for her and following along as she experienced the city for the first time. He'd forgotten what an adventure New Orleans could be, taken his home for granted for far too long. Simply seeing the awe in her eyes sent a tiny thrill of life humming through his veins.

"What kind do you want?"

He stood against the wall, inhaling the scents of sweet cream and warm waffle cones, unable to remember the last time he'd had ice cream. "None for me, thank you."

She cocked one hip to the side, resting her hand on it. "If it's about money, I've got loads of it, so don't worry."

"It's not about money, though I do need to work again sometime soon if I'm going to pay the bills."

"What would I do while you worked?"

"I suppose I'd have to take you with me until you get your license." Not that he would get much done with her hanging around the office, talking constantly.

"What kind of work do you do?"

"I'm an accountant. I do temp work here and there." Just enough to get by. The rest of the time he spent alone in his home. In fact, he'd been out more in the two weeks he'd known Jane than he had in the past ten years.

She lifted her hands. "Oh, no. I'm not sitting in a stuffy office all night while you crunch numbers. Your job right now is to take care of me—which is a stupid law, and I'm only letting you because you'd probably be staked if I didn't—so I'll pay the bills."

He crossed his arms. "I don't need you to pay my bills." Nor did he want her to.

She tapped a finger against her lips, looking thoughtful and too damn cute again. "I know. My brother has been managing my accounts, but I can transfer them to you. I'll bring in the money. You manage it. We'll be a perfect team." She stepped up to the counter and ordered a cone of mint chocolate chip.

He couldn't imagine Jane Anderson wanting to be a part of anyone's team, though he had to admit the idea sounded appealing. He was starting to enjoy spending time with her. But it was enjoyment he didn't deserve. No, he and Jane could never be a team.

"What kind do you want, Ethan? Don't make me eat alone."

He sighed. "It has no nutritional value."

"It never has." She grinned and licked the blob of ice cream sitting atop her cone.

Heat pooled in his groin, and his dick hardened as the image of her tongue sliding across his skin flashed behind his eyes. How could he say no to her when she affected him this way? "Surprise me."

She placed the order and handed him a cone. "You look like a dark chocolate kind of guy. Deep and smooth, with just a little bit of a bite."

He took a lick, and creamy, sweet chocolate danced on his taste buds, making him shiver. Closing his eyes, he took another bite and savored the decadent sensation. He always drank warm blood. It had been ages since something cool had slid down his throat.

He opened his eyes to find Jane biting her lip, watching him with a fire in her eyes. Damn, he wanted her. He couldn't deny her allure, but he refused to give in. A happy life was not in the cards for him. Not after what he'd done to Vanessa.

He stiffened, stomping out of the ice cream shop and onto Decatur before he could drown in the depths of her gaze.

She hurried to catch up. "Did I say something wrong?"

"No." He stalked forward, tossing his half-eaten cone in a trash can.

"Why do you do that?"

He clenched his fists, continuing his march. "What do I do?"

"We've been together twenty-four-seven for two straight weeks. Every now and then, you start opening up...being *nice* to me, letting me know Ethan, and then, bam. The gates slam down, and Edward Cullen is back. What gives?" She jogged. "And slow down. I'm not as fast as you."

He whirled to face her. "You would be if you'd feed." If she would get her damn license he could be done with her and away from the temptation.

She flinched. "Yeah, well, I don't want to. And no one makes Jane Anderson do anything she doesn't want to do."

He lifted his hands, dropping them by his sides. "You're impossible."

"So are you."

A woman tripped on the curb in front of them, falling to her knees before her elbows scraped across the pavement. The coppery scent of fresh blood mixed with the warm, earthy tones of spiced rum, and despite his efforts, Ethan's fangs extended. He clamped his mouth shut and gripped Jane's arm as the woman stood and examined the blood dripping down her elbow. Surely the enticing aroma would do Jane in. Her fangs were probably fully extended as well. He had to get her away before she lunged for the woman.

Jane froze, her nose crinkling as the ice cream slipped from her grasp, splatting on the sidewalk. "Blood," she murmured before her eyes rolled back and she crumpled to the ground.

Without a second thought, he scooped her into his arms and marched her to his car parked in the lot near the river. Her eyes fluttered open as he positioned her in the passenger seat and buckled the seat belt around her.

"Oh, man. Sorry about that." She clutched her head.

He squatted beside the car. "This has gone on long enough. You need blood."

"I saw enough blood tonight, thank you."

He shook his head, frustration gnawing at his chest. "You need to consume it."

"Why am I in the car? Where are we going?"

He slammed the door and stomped around to the driver's side, yanking on the handle. "To see Sophie. Maybe she can talk some sense into you, because I am done, Jane."

Her mouth fell open. "Done? You can't be done."

"Your stubbornness is killing you and making me miserable in the process."

"I can't die, and you're already miserable." She inclined her chin.

"You're wasting away, and you *know* what the punishment will be if you don't get your license."

"Still can't get your girl to feed?" Gaston smirked as he approached.

If Ethan had been paying attention, he'd have sensed his sire's proximity, but he was so torn between his concern for Jane's health and his desire to choke her, he couldn't think of anything else. "Aside from force-feeding her, I don't know what else to do."

"Well, I bring two pieces of information. First, I want

to tell Miss Jane that her request has been completed." He leaned down and looked at her in the car.

"Thank you, Gaston. You're the best." She smiled and laid her head back on the headrest, closing her eyes.

"She doesn't look well," Gaston said as he straightened.

"She's not. What was her request?"

He chuckled. "I'm not at liberty to divulge that information, my friend. Get her healthy, and then I'm sure she'll tell you."

He didn't have the strength nor the patience to argue. "What's the other thing?"

"Oh, yes. You've both been summoned by the Council. They want to see you tomorrow evening."

His heart sank. He couldn't let them see her in this condition. They'd probably stake him for being the crappiest sire in existence. "About what?" She had another week left on her permit. They didn't need to see her now.

"That I do not know, my friend, but I suggest you get some blood in her before you arrive. Neglect of your offspring is punishable by stake."

Every damn thing was punishable by stake these days. He said goodbye to Gaston, got in the driver's seat, and sped toward Esplanade Avenue to Sophie's rental house. Jane sagged into his side as he guided her up the front steps and banged on the door.

A few minutes later, Sophie's grumbling voice filtered through the wood. "I know y'all keep undead hours, but this human needs her beauty sleep." She swung open the door, and her eyes widened. "What happened to her?"

He scooped Jane into his arms and carried her into the living room, laying her on the sofa. "She passed out. A woman was bleeding, and I think this fasting is too much for her. I expected her to lunge toward the blood, but instead, she hit the ground."

Sophie darted into the kitchen and returned with a wet rag. "She hasn't told you why she won't drink blood?"

"No. Just that Jane Anderson refuses to do anything she doesn't want to do."

She tilted her head, giving him a sympathetic look. "She faints at the sight of it. Always has."

He paused, blinking a few times as her words sank in. "Please tell me you're kidding. A vampire who faints at the sight of blood?"

"I wish I were."

He dragged his hands down his face. No wonder she was so adamant about not learning to feed. Every time he'd tried to demonstrate, she'd turned her head the moment his fangs met flesh.

"We've been summoned to the Council tomorrow. I can't take her there in this condition, and, well…I'm worried about her health. Will you talk to her? She won't listen to me."

Sophie knelt beside the couch and dabbed the rag on Jane's head. "Listen, babe, you've got to drink some blood."

Jane shook her head. "Never."

"Look at you. You're a fucking *vampire* with a black belt in karate. You're a badass. An immortal. You don't want to live all eternity like this, do you? And, frankly…" She leaned closer to her ear and whispered, "You're shriveling up like a raisin. I think I see crow's feet."

"I can't do it, Soph. Will you get me some water? My throat's on fire."

Sophie sighed and stood, jerking her head toward the hallway before strutting to the back of the house.

Ethan followed. "What am I going to do? I can't stand to see her suffering like this, and if the Council finds out she refuses to feed, they'll stake us both for her incompetence."

"Okay, at first you had me believing you actually cared about her…until the incompetence line."

He rubbed his forehead. "I do care about her. More than I planned to." And wasn't that the devil's honest truth? No matter how infuriating the woman was, he was into her. *Really* into her.

"Can she hear us?" Sophie asked.

"Possibly."

"Come outside with me. I have a plan." She opened the back door and strutted onto the porch. "Can you drink blood not straight from a person? Like, can you put it in a cup?"

"Sure, but it's still blood. If she can't stomach it from the vein—"

She held up a hand. "Listen, Jane is stubborn as all get-out. She always has been, and she's used to getting what she wants."

He crossed his arms. "I hadn't noticed."

"Sometimes what Jane wants and what Jane needs aren't the same things. Then, you have to get creative."

"I'm listening."

"Can you get some blood? I don't want to know how, but can you bring some here?"

"Sure." The Blood Bank wasn't far, and he had a line of credit there. "I can get a pint or two."

"Great. However much you think she needs, put it in a Styrofoam cup with a lid and a straw. We're going to trick her."

"Do you think that will work?"

Sophie shrugged. "If she needs it that badly, she won't be able to stop once she starts, right?"

"I suppose she won't. It will instantly soothe her throat." But Jane was smart. He couldn't see her being fooled easily. "If I bring her a random drink, she'll suspect."

"No, she won't. She trusts me. You get the blood, and I'll convince her to drink it."

He nodded. "Give me half an hour."

Jane squeezed her eyes shut against the overhead lights and nestled deeper into the sofa. If only the damn thing would open up and swallow her whole, putting her out of her misery. That ice cream didn't help her throat a bit, and now Ethan was mad at her for no apparent reason. Her head pounded, and she was so damn thirsty, she could have drunk the entire Mississippi River.

"All right." Sophie shuffled into the room. "I sent that man of yours out to get you a miracle cure. It's the only thing that will help you."

"Miracle cure?" She opened her eyes and squinted. "Can you turn off the lights?"

"Sure." Sophie flipped the switch and turned on an end table lamp instead. "Remember the drink we had that cured our hangovers?"

"Oh yeah." She'd forgotten how much better that one little drink made her feel. But that was a hangover; this was a dire need for a substance she couldn't stand to look at, much less ingest. "Do you think it will help?"

"It's worth a try."

"Okay." She pushed to sitting, folding her legs beneath her. "Is he still mad at me?"

Sophie sank onto the cushion next to her. "Why would he be mad at you?"

"I don't know. We were talking and getting along, and then he just shut down. I don't know what I did."

Sophie grinned. "He's not mad. Frustrated, but not mad."

"What are you smiling at?"

She folded her hands in her lap. "You care."

"So?"

"You normally don't give a damn if someone gets mad at you, but you care about Ethan, and he cares about you. It's so cute to watch this little relationship blooming."

Jane shook her head. "He only cares so he can get me a biting license and be done with me."

"That's not true." A knock sounded on the door. "He went all the way to the French Quarter to get your miracle cure. He likes you."

Sophie opened the door, and Ethan came in carrying a Styrofoam cup. He handed it to Sophie before sinking into a chair and fisting his hands in his lap. Always fisting.

"Here you go." Sophie passed the cup to Jane. "One miracle cure to remedy your woes."

Jane examined the cup, plain white with a dark red straw. "Did it come from the same bar? It might not work otherwise."

Sophie looked over her shoulder at Ethan. "You got it from the place we talked about, right?"

His fists clenched tighter. "I did precisely what you told me to do."

"It's exactly what you need, hon. Drink up." Sophie pushed the cup toward Jane's face.

"Okay, okay. Here goes nothing." She touched the straw to her lips and took a giant sip, hoping the first gulp would be enough to extinguish the fire in her throat. She cringed at the metallic taste—like someone had dropped an entire roll of pennies in her drink—but as soon as the liquid slid down her throat, the inferno in her esophagus cooled like a glacier sliding over the flames.

She knew this was blood. It couldn't be anything but. And her mind wanted her to choke, to throw the cup across the room and curse them both for tricking her. But her body took over, instinct forcing her to chug the entire contents of the container.

"Whoa. Slow down and breathe." Sophie put a hand on her shoulder.

"She technically doesn't need to," Ethan said.

Sophie's eyes held concern as Jane sat up straight and set the cup on the coffee table. "How do you feel?"

Jane looked at Ethan. Apprehension etched lines into his forehead, and his fists were clenched so tight, his pale skin had gone completely white around his knuckles.

She rolled her neck, running a hand over her throat because she couldn't believe how instantly it had healed. But the most miraculous thing? She'd just ingested sixteen ounces of human blood, and she didn't feel the slightest bit lightheaded.

Scooting to the edge of the couch, she slowly stood, expecting her normal reaction to overcome her any second and send her crumbling to the floor. It didn't happen. She felt fine. Better than fine—she felt amazing.

"You both think you're real smart for tricking me like that, don't you? I know that was blood in that cup." She fisted her hands on her hips, fighting her smile and glaring at them both.

Ethan's hands relaxed on his knees, his entire demeanor shifting as his posture softened. One corner of his mouth tugged into an almost-grin—the closest thing she'd seen to a smile on the man since the day he turned her—and he rose to his feet. "Technically, Sophie did the tricking. I merely acquired the provisions."

Sophie laughed. "'Acquired the provisions.' He's funny."

"He's definitely something." She smiled at Ethan, and when he looked back at her, she got the overwhelming urge to throw herself into his arms and show him just how much she appreciated his efforts to keep her functioning. Instead, she hugged Sophie. "Thanks for everything."

"He's good for you," she whispered back.

"I know." She shuffled to the door. "Well, I guess this settles the license issue. I can drink blood from a straw, so I'll never have to bite anyone."

Ethan's almost-smile faded. "I have no issues with buying you blood. I keep a supply in my fridge anyway, but the law states everyone within one hundred miles of a city must have a license…whether you're biting or not. The Council has every right to stake you if you don't."

Jane took his hand. "Let me worry about the Council. Right now, we need to get home. I've got something to show you."

CHAPTER NINE

Relief flooded Ethan's body, the sensation making him lightheaded as he drove up Dauphine toward his home in Bywater. Small Creole cottages in pastel shades lined the narrow street, and his Ford lurched as he hit two potholes in a row.

Jane bubbled with excitement in the seat next to him. What she could possibly want to show him that had her this worked up, he couldn't fathom, but seeing her happy…and healthy again…sent a zing through his chest, sparking life in his undead heart.

If it weren't for that stupid law, and especially that damn British constable, Jane might actually stand a chance of survival. She may have had the upper hand with people in human politics, but she was clueless when it came to the inner workings of the supernatural world.

"I have an idea," he said as he made a right on Gallier. "Gourds."

Jane gave him a quizzical look. "You mean, like pumpkins? What about them?"

"Yes. Yellow squash would probably be a good place to

start, though. Or zucchini."

She laughed. "What on Earth are you talking about?"

"To practice biting. The consistency is similar. The flesh of the gourd would have a similar give, and you could—"

"I don't need to learn biting techniques. I can buy my meals from the bank. Or, rather, I can give you the money, and you can buy them. I doubt I could step foot inside the place. Do they have the blood on display? Like bags hanging from hooks in a refrigerated case? Or is it kept in a tank?" She shivered. "Never mind. Don't answer that."

He reached for her hand across the console. "I know you think you can convince the Council to bend the law for you, but..."

She placed her free hand on top of his. "I *know* I can."

He bit back a growl of frustration. "Okay, but even if you do convince them, will you humor me? Let me teach you the technique just in case the situation ever arises where you might be forced to?"

She fake-smiled and tapped her canine tooth. "I don't have fangs."

"You can still learn." He squeezed her hand and slipped from her grasp as he rolled to a stop and turned off the engine.

Jane twisted in her seat to face him. "Would it make you happy if I did?"

"Very."

"Okay. Gourds it is, but let's start with zucchini. I don't like yellow squash unless it's fried." She opened the car door. "Now, come on. I can't wait for you to see this."

He followed as she pranced up the walk, bouncing on her toes as she waited for him to let her inside. Damn, she was cute when she was excited.

"What are you so worked up about?"

"You'll see. Open the door." She pushed it open the moment the lock disengaged and zipped inside at vampire speed—finally. Whoever donated the pint she consumed must've been a heavy coffee drinker. He stepped through the threshold and closed the door.

"Are you ready?" If she got any more excited, she'd explode.

"As I'll ever be."

She giggled and flipped a switch on the wall…a switch he was certain had never been there before. Machinery hummed to life, and blackout screens lowered over all the windows, locking into place in unison as a metal barrier rose up from the floor, blocking the door. She'd equipped his home with the most state-of-the-art vampire protection system on the market. The simple systems cost a fortune, but this…

He stepped toward a window and ran his finger along the rubber seal. This system was built for fortresses. For royalty. For…

"Well?" She clasped her hands together in front of her chest and looked at him with wide, wondrous eyes. "What do you think?"

"I…" His jaw trembled, so he snapped his mouth shut. It was too much. How could he accept such an extravagant gift when all he'd done for her was damn her to darkness?

"It's great, isn't it? Now we don't have to sleep in the attic."

"I can't accept this, Jane."

Her smile faded. "Why not? It's the least I could do to show my appreciation."

He raked a hand through his hair. "Your appreciation

for what? I damned you."

"You saved my life."

"By turning you into a monster."

She crossed her arms. "We are not monsters, Edward. Now take a hike and bring Ethan back. I like him a lot better."

"How much did all of this cost?"

"It doesn't matter, and anyway…it's not just for you. Jane Anderson does not belong in a dusty old attic."

"That's true. You don't." Leave it to Jane to turn his pity party around and defuse all his arguments by making it about her.

"So…what do you really think?"

"I…" This woman never ceased to amaze him. "I love it. Thank you."

"There's more," she sang as she took his hand and led him down the hall to the master bedroom. "Your twenty-five-year-old mattress was full of dust, so I bought you a new one. The sheets were toast too, so I got a new set. Emerald to match your eyes. If you don't like it, I can have Sophie return it tomorrow."

"It's perfect." It seemed his initial impression of Jane had been all wrong. She wasn't the selfish, entitled princess he'd originally pegged her for. She was thoughtful, and while she still talked way too much, he'd grown fond of the sound of her voice and the little blast of electricity he felt every time she touched him.

"Oh. My. Goat cheese." She parked her hands on her hips and cocked her head. "You're smiling."

"I am not." He tried to flatten his lips into a neutral expression, but it was no use. The woman had gotten to him.

"Yes, you are." Her grin could have burned the entire

coven to ash. "Does this mean brooding Edward is gone for good, and Ethan is here to stay?"

He chuckled. "I'm not making any promises."

"I hope you'll find reasons to smile more often. It looks good on you." She looked into his eyes, and he looked into hers, and that hollow spot in his chest that had been there since he removed the mating mark started to ache.

"Oh, I almost forgot." She grabbed his hand and tugged him to the next room. "I know I get on your nerves, and since you're not allowed to get rid of me during waking hours…" She pushed open the door to reveal a queen-sized bed with a deep purple duvet. "I figured I'd give you a little space at bedtime at least."

"But that's the only time you're tolerable." He winked.

She flipped her hair behind her shoulders. "I'm growing on you. Admit it."

"Maybe a little." Or a lot. He was getting used to having her around, that was for sure. There hadn't been a dull moment since he turned her.

Her face went serious. "So, this meeting with the Council tomorrow. Are we in trouble?"

"I honestly have no idea, but it's probably best if you let me do the talking." She opened her mouth to protest, but he lifted a finger to quiet her…and it actually worked. "Stay silent in the beginning, until we see what the issue is. Once they've said their piece, then you can turn on your charm, okay?"

She nodded. "Deal. Well, I can feel that the sun will be up soon. We better get some rest."

He stilled, opening his senses to the atmosphere. Sunrise wasn't for another half-hour, but young vampires could barely keep their eyes open during early daylight hours. She'd be dragged down into the death sleep shortly after morning broke.

Moving toward her, he opened his arms, and she stepped into them as if she belonged in his embrace. "Thank you, Jane."

She hugged him tightly and stepped away, a look of uncertainty clouding her eyes. "You're welcome. See you tomorrow." Slipping inside the bedroom, she closed the door, leaving him alone in the hall.

Alone. It was all he'd wanted since the night she woke up as a vampire, but now that his treasured silence had returned, it was deafening.

He shuffled to his bedroom and stripped down to his boxer briefs, something he hadn't been able to do since he met Jane. Lifting the blanket, he slid beneath the sheets and stared at the ceiling fan hanging stagnant above him.

Ten minutes later, a soft knock sounded, and Jane hesitated in his doorway. She wore pale pink flannel boxer shorts and a cream-colored tank top nearly the same color as her skin.

He rose onto his elbows. "Something wrong, princess?"

She bit her bottom lip and padded to the foot of the bed. "This whole being *dead to the world* thing is scary alone. I've never done it without you."

The vulnerability in her eyes nearly tore him two. So Jane Anderson wasn't invincible after all. He pulled the sheets down. "Want to join me?"

"Do you mind?"

He shrugged. "I've gotten used to falling asleep with you too. Though I better warn you, I'm only wearing my underwear."

A tiny smile tilted her lips. "I promise to behave

myself." She hopped into bed and snuggled under the covers, turning on her side to face him. "Can I ask you a personal question?"

He rolled over to face her. "Ask me anything."

"How did Vanessa die?"

He closed his eyes and chewed the inside of his cheek. Why did she have to bring up his past when he was just starting to enjoy the present? He tried to roll onto his back, but she caught his hand, clutching it tightly in hers.

"Don't shut down on me. Please, I want to know you."

With a long exhale, he opened his eyes and met her pleading gaze. "It was my fault. I killed her."

Her mouth dropped open, horrified. "Did you drain her?"

"No. It happened before I was turned. We got in an argument, and…" He shook his head. She didn't really want to hear this.

She took his other hand, lacing their fingers together. "What happened? What was the argument about?"

"It was Halloween. She wanted me to go to this costume party with her dressed as a Thing One and Thing Two. Blue wigs and all. It was a couple's costume, but I refused to wear it. It was ridiculous, and I don't do costumes to begin with, but I… I should have. I should have just worn the damn thing."

She scooted closer until their arms touched from hands to elbows. "You don't strike me as a costume-wearing kind of man."

"I told her the only way I'd go to the party was without the costume. She agreed, but we argued the whole time. We started doing shots, trying to outdrink each other." His jaw clenched. "It was so stupid. I don't know what we were thinking. What *I* was thinking."

"Did you have to Uber home?"

"Uber didn't exist back then. When it was time to leave, she insisted on driving. I should have taken the keys, called a taxi, or… My tolerance was so much higher than hers, but I was so sick of fighting, I let her get behind the wheel." His gaze lost focus, and he stared blankly at their entwined hands. "We ran off the road and hit a tree. I survived. She didn't."

"I'm so sorry."

"If I'd made her let me drive. Hell, if I'd worn the stupid costume, it wouldn't have happened. She would still be alive."

"Maybe. Or maybe if *you'd* driven, you'd both be dead now. You don't know."

"Death would be better than the past twenty-five years of my life," he mumbled.

"Don't say that. You don't mean that." She tightened her grip on his hands. "Alcohol messes with your head, believe me. You both made bad decisions, but you couldn't have known what would happen. You can't keep beating yourself up for a past you can't change."

"I know. Believe me, I've thought about it for twenty-five years, but it's easier to hate myself for it. I haven't let myself really live since she died." He met her gaze. "Until now."

"It's been long enough, don't you think? Don't you want to move on? Let it go?"

"I do. I am trying. I just haven't had anything to live for until now."

She pressed her lips together, lowering her gaze, not taking the hint, not hearing what he wasn't able to say. "I know you wanted me to be Vanessa. I'm sorry I'm not her."

"I'm not." He lifted her chin with a finger. "Sometimes, the things we want aren't the same as what we need. I'm glad you're you, Jane Anderson. You are exactly what I need."

"Aren't you sweet?" She leaned toward him and pressed a kiss to his cheek.

His heart thumped, and she lingered there, slowly pulling back, her nose gliding along his skin until her lips were a scant half-inch from his mouth. Her gaze flicked to his, and she swallowed hard, hesitating as if asking his permission.

He tilted his head, brushing his bottom lip against her top, and that was all the invitation she needed. Reaching a hand to his face, she crushed her mouth to his. It had been so long since he'd kissed a woman, he was afraid he'd forget what to do, but the moment Jane's tongue slipped between his lips, it all came back to him.

His fangs extended, a normal reaction to sexual attraction—or so Gaston had assured him—and his dick hardened like a steel rod. Jane moaned, gripping the back of his head to tug him closer, but then she pulled away, gasping as if she'd lost her breath.

"It's morning." She touched her lips with trembling fingers. "I can't stay awake."

"Then go to sleep, princess. I'll be here."

She smiled, and, brushing one more gentle kiss to his lips, she rolled over, snuggling her back against his front, his rock-hard dick pressing against her ass. "Oh, my. I'm sorry I'm going to miss out on that."

He chuckled. "You're not the only one. Sweet dreams, sweet Jane."

She yawned. "See ya later, alligator." Then she went still as a corpse, the death sleep overtaking her.

CHAPTER TEN

E than sat on the sofa, staring at the blank TV screen while last night's kiss played on a loop in his mind. He'd been awake for nearly an hour before Jane began to stir, but he'd only allowed himself to remain by her side for ten minutes before he rose and dressed for the evening.

He'd caught a glimpse of her scurrying down the hall to the shower, but she hadn't emerged from her bedroom since she entered it half an hour ago.

Her Styrofoam cup, filled with blood, sat on the coffee table, and as footsteps sounded from the hallway, Ethan rose to his feet.

She appeared in the living room wearing black leggings and a long, burgundy sweater with a deep V-neck that revealed the delicate curve of her neck and the sweet swell of her breasts. She looked good enough to eat.

"Good morning…er…evening, I guess." She tousled her dark hair and smiled softly. "Sleep well?"

"Like the dead." He offered her the cup. "Breakfast?"

"Thanks." She shuffled into the living room and took the cup from his hand. Pausing, she grimaced and stared at the straw. "I know I need this, but my mind won't let me."

He knew the feeling. "Pretend it's vodka and tomato juice. Your miracle cure."

She chuckled and lifted the cup in a toast. "Breakfast of champions." Pressing the straw to her lips, she took a quick sip, which turned into a huge gulp, and within seconds, she'd downed the entire contents. "Damn, that's good."

His tongue slipped out to moisten his lips against his will, and her gaze flicked to his mouth.

"Listen...about last night." She set the cup on the table. "I'm sorry?"

He cocked his head. "Why did you say it like a question?"

She shrugged. "I guess because I'm really not. But it seemed like the thing to say in a situation like this."

"What situation?"

"I don't know." She flung her arms in the air and dropped them at her sides. "Why are you making this hard on me? We kissed last night, and now we have to talk about it, right? That's how these things go."

He fought a grin. She was adorable when she was flustered. "So, you're not sorry you kissed me?"

She crossed her arms, cocking a brow. "That depends on how you feel about it."

"I enjoyed it, personally. Quite a lot, actually."

She giggled and glanced at his pants. "I remember. Vlad wanted to come out and play."

He opened his mouth to respond, but as her words sank in, he paused. "Did you just name my dick Vlad?"

"It's fitting. If the death sleep hadn't pulled me under, I might have let him impale me."

He shook his head, a deep chuckle vibrating in his chest. "Oh, Jane. What am I going to do with you?"

"I can think of a few things." She bit her lip and gazed at him for a moment. "We're still cool then? Things aren't going to get awkward now?"

"I really hope not."

"Then why do you still look worried?" She pointed at his face. "Your brow is pinched, and you keep clenching and unclenching your fists."

He shoved his hands in his pockets. Damn, this woman was perceptive.

"Are you worried about the Council?"

"I am. The only reason I can think that they would call us back would be about your biter's license. We haven't done anything illegal…that I'm aware of."

She raised her hands. "Don't look at me like that. I haven't left your side since I died." She chewed her bottom lip, her face scrunching the way it always did when she was deep in thought. "Do you trust me, Ethan?"

"Of course." His answer came without hesitation, taking him by surprise. He did trust Jane. With every fiber of his being.

She smiled. "I trust you too. So get the Council warmed up, get them to give me *permission* to speak." She stuck her finger in her mouth, making a gagging motion. "Then I'll handle it from there. My ability to schmooze will amaze you."

"If you try to use even a smidge of glamour on them, they'll sense it. Using glamour against the Council is punishable by stake."

She rolled her eyes. "Cheese and crackers, everything is *punishable by stake* with you guys. You need a woman on the Council. That's what you need. How do you get elected? I'll make a run for it, and being a vampire will be fun again."

He chuckled. "You have to be at least fifty years dead to even be considered."

"Damn. Well, it's never too early to start campaigning."

Ethan rolled his neck, attempting to stretch the tension from his shoulders, but as soon as he stopped, they crept back toward his ears. He sat on the sofa in the sitting-room of the coven's headquarters, holding on to Jane's hand as if she were his lifeline. If he'd done something to get her into trouble, he'd never forgive himself.

"Relax." She put her free hand on top of his. "We've got this."

"You underestimate the power and temperament of the Council."

"You underestimate the power and temperament of Jane Anderson. We're going to be fine."

"I hope you're right."

"I got you to smile yesterday. That in itself is a feat worthy of recognition."

The door creaked open, and Jeffrey, a squat man with blond hair and a bushy mustache, stepped through. "You may enter."

Ethan's heart crept into his throat. His entire death, he'd kept his head down, stayed out of politics, and minded his own business. He rarely socialized with anyone, including other vampires, and he'd managed to stay out of trouble because of it. Until Jane, he'd only been summoned to the Council twice

—once to get his biter's permit, and then again for his license.

He'd heard stories of vampires who'd been randomly called before the Council, and holy Satan's balls, he hoped they were only stories.

With Jane's hand clutched tightly in his, they crept down the hallway and entered the Council's chamber. All five members donned their robes and sat perched atop their thrones. Off to the side, Watson, the British constable, sat in his own ornate chair, like a little kid's version of a throne. Who did this guy think he was?

"What's with the man-child?" Jane's voice echoed in his head.

"I think he wants the Magistrate's job. How did you send me your thoughts? I haven't taught you to do that."

Her eyes sparkled. *"I'm full of surprises."*

"That you are."

"There's that smile, again. It really does look good on you."

They stopped in the center of the room, and Ethan lowered his head in a bow, squeezing Jane's hand to remind her to do the same. Thankfully, she followed his lead. The Magistrate shuffled through a stack of papers as if he'd lost the one he needed.

"They don't have their files digitized?" Jane's voice drifted through his mind.

"I told you they're old school here. Now stop thought-talking before you get us both staked."

She laughed softly. *"I can't wait to shake things up in this place."*

"Ethan Devereaux," the Magistrate's voice boomed.

He swallowed, willing his heart to dislodge from his throat and settle in his chest where it belonged. "Yes, Your Honor?"

"It has come to my attention that your recently-turned subject belongs to the Governor of Texas."

Jane opened her mouth, sucking in a breath to protest the Magistrate's use of the word "belong," Ethan assumed. He squeezed her hand and sent her a mental message: "*Let it go, Elsa.*" She pursed her lips.

"She is the Governor's daughter, Your Honor. A fact I was unaware of at the time." His heart willingly fell from his throat, plopping into his stomach. That's what this summoning was about? That Ethan turned someone of high importance, so now *he* was in trouble?

Constable Watson wiggled in his chair like an overly excited puppy. The bastard probably carried pickets inside his trench coat just in case he got the chance to stake someone.

"Turning people in her position of power is…" The Magistrate glanced at Watson. "It's frowned upon."

The constable shot to his feet. "The Supernatural World Order has decreed it can't be done without filing the proper paperwork first. You've committed a crime, Mr. Devereaux. It's time to pay the price." He brushed back his jacket, and sure enough, a set of stakes were attached to the underside.

"Now hold on a second." Jane slipped from his grasp and strutted forward. "He saved my life; how can that be considered a crime? Don't y'all have some kind of Good Samaritan law or something?" She glared at Watson.

"Calm down, or we'll both be staked."

She glanced at Ethan. "*Neither one of us is getting staked on my watch.*"

The Magistrate scanned Jane's registration papers. "She has a good point." He passed them down the line of

Council members. "She'd been struck by a car and would have died otherwise."

The men murmured amongst themselves, and Ethan wished it mattered that he held his breath. The pain in his chest would have been a nice distraction from his impending death.

"Honestly, gentlemen, Ethan did us all a favor," Jane said. "The state of Louisiana wouldn't want to have the blood of the Texas Governor's daughter on its hands. Imagine the drama that would have caused. The humans owe you one now, if you ask me."

"Go on." The Magistrate leaned forward.

"You've got a bargaining chip now, one you can use with both Louisiana and Texas. I absolutely love being a vampire, so the next time one of ours gets into a tiff with the humans, you can remind them that you saved my life, and I'm thankful for it. I know my father. He'd rather have me around as a vampire than buried six feet under."

"Are you sure about that?" Ethan asked in Jane's mind.

"Absolutely, and I'll tell him everything when the time is right. You'll see."

Ethan watched in awe as Jane schmoozed the men in the room—all but Watson, of course—convincing them Ethan's turning her hadn't broken a law he wasn't even aware existed. By the time she finished her speech, they were all nodding in agreement.

The Magistrate rapped his gavel on the table in front of him. "Ethan Devereaux, you are acquitted of all charges and are to be commended for your efforts to save this woman's life."

The constable shot to his feet. "Preposterous! What's next? Will you allow someone to turn the President? I cannot let this go unpunished."

"You have no authority here." The Magistrate's pupils narrowed to slits, his irises glowing red. "You're nothing but a messenger for the Emperor of the SWO, who allows his Magistrates to interpret the laws and hand out punishment as they see fit."

Watson sank into his baby throne. "She should at least be sent back to Texas where she belongs. This coven doesn't need to stir up any more issues with the humans."

"You want me here, Magistrate." Jane turned on the charm. "Think of it. The Governor's daughter, a vampire, willingly living in Louisiana. I could be a liaison…a bridge between the states as well as the human and vampire governments." She flipped her hair behind her shoulder. "I'm the best thing that's ever happened to supernatural New Orleans."

Ethan tensed, waiting for the Magistrate to unleash his wrath at her statement, but the man simply nodded, his lips curving as he considered her words.

"You may be right, young lady." The old man winked —actually winked—at Ethan. "I like her."

"You have good reason to, sir." He clasped his hands behind his back and let Jane continue her magic.

"I have a few ideas I'd like to run by you while I have your ear, sir." She leaned forward and lowered her voice. "But I'd rather not discuss it in front of outsiders." She nodded toward the constable.

"Give us the room, Watson," the Magistrate said.

"But—"

"I said leave." He hissed as Watson cinched his coat closed and scurried out the door. "Good call getting rid of the weasel, Ms. Anderson. He was getting on my nerves."

Her smile could have lit an entire city block. She went on to propose an idea for a nightclub where patrons paid a cover charge to be bitten by vampires. "Everyone knows there are vampires in New Orleans, but most people—myself included, until I met Ethan—think they're just humans with a few screws loose who like to play pretend and drink real blood."

She shuddered. "Of course, our vampires will be the real deal, and they can use their glamour to make it a pleasant...possibly erotic...experience for the donors. I haven't worked out all the details, but people will be lined up around the block to experience a bit of the darker side of the Big Easy."

The idea made sense, but when had she thought all this up? It was the first Ethan had heard of it.

"I'm happy to oversee the operations...behind the scenes. I know how to throw a party. Think of all the revenue it would bring in. You'd have more bargaining power with the humans and...whoever else you bargain with."

"It's a fabulous idea." The Magistrate clapped his hands. "Your new subject is proving herself indispensable, Mr. Devereaux. Good choice."

"Thank you, sir. She is pretty amazing."

"Wonderful. Oh, Ms. Anderson, since you're here, would you like to test for your biter's license and save yourself a trip? It's the least I can offer for your advantageous ideas."

She pressed her lips together and looked at Ethan. He lifted his brow and spoke in her mind: "*Turn the charm back on, princess. They've been staking people for this for weeks already.*"

Straightening her spine, she lifted her chin and explained her issue with blood. "I'm sure if Ethan had known, he wouldn't have turned me, but he didn't, so here we are. I have plenty of income to buy what I need from your bank, so I'll be contributing to society monetarily. But there's simply no way I could bite a person, Your Honor. Not anytime soon. Would you be so kind as to give me an extension on my permit?"

The Magistrate steepled his fingers, glancing about the room as if making sure Watson didn't sneak back inside. "Three weeks, just to spite that little shit, and you mention this to no one. If word gets out that I've gone soft on you, that weasel will report me to the SWO and have me removed."

"Thank you, sir. I won't utter a word of it. New Orleans is lucky to have you as a leader, and I would never do anything to jeopardize your position." She glanced over her shoulder at Ethan and winked.

The Magistrate nodded. "This city has thrived under my rule for the last hundred years. Then that weasel Watson shows up with his Supernatural World Order mandates, and all hell breaks loose. He's staked four of my people already."

She gasped, placing a hand on her chest. "A tragedy."

"Indeed."

Wow. This two-week-dead vampire was talking with the Magistrate like they were old friends. *The Magistrate.* The man who struck fear into the hearts of every vampire in the city...except for maybe Gaston. He was too drunk to be afraid. Never in Ethan's twenty-five years as a vampire had he seen someone take command with her superiors like this.

She was fierce, intelligent, incredibly savvy, and insanely beautiful on top of it all. Vlad had stood up and taken notice. It was time Ethan did too.

The Magistrate dismissed them, and as they exited the

coven headquarters, thunder clapped from above. A static charge built in the air, and ominous dark clouds gathered in the night sky.

His elation at their—at Jane's—accomplishment quickly tumbled into darkness, his mood growing grimmer than the brothers themselves. They had to get home, out of the storm.

CHAPTER ELEVEN

Jane followed Ethan up the front steps and waited as he unlocked the door. He'd been quiet on the way home, nervously glancing at the sky as if he were afraid it would open up and swallow him whole. No doubt, he was in shock at the way she'd handled the Council tonight. He'd doubted her, but Jane had grown up in politics; she knew how to stroke egos. Vampires were no different than men in that arena.

He fumbled with the key, dropping it on the porch and cursing before picking it up and jabbing it into the lock.

"Are you okay?" She put her hand on his arm, and he tensed.

"Yeah. Just want to get inside before the rain starts."

She laughed. "Don't tell me we'll melt. That's just witches, right?"

Lightning flashed in the distance, and thunder boomed as he threw the door open and marched inside. "No one melts in the rain, Jane."

She ignored his irritated tone and followed him into

the living room as rain fell from the sky. "We were brilliant in there tonight. What did you think about my idea for the vampire bar? I came up with it on the fly, but I think it could really work. I won't be able to travel for my blog much, so I'll need to supplement my income. I could totally run a night club, as long as I don't have to watch anyone actually biting people. I'd call the evening a success, wouldn't you?"

His hands curled into fists like they always did when he wasn't happy—which was often. "You only got a three-week extension on your permit. You still have to get over your aversion to blood."

"Oh, pish." She waved her hand dismissively. "I'll get it extended indefinitely. I didn't want to push too far tonight. Don't worry."

"Whatever you say." He flipped the switch to close the light-blocking blinds and plopped onto the sofa, his expression going from grim to confused and back again.

She turned the switch back up, raising the blinds. "Sunrise isn't for another three hours. Let's enjoy the storm."

"I do not enjoy storms." He shot to his feet and hit the switch again, sending the blinds back down.

"What's not to love about them? The energy in the air alone is fantastic, and I adore the sound of rain falling on the roof, rapping against the windows. It's so relaxing." She waited for him to step away from the switch before she hit it again.

"This is my house, and I want them closed," he growled before tapping the switch and covering it with his hand.

"Oh, wow." Jane raised her hands. "I see how it is. It's your house, and you want the blinds *that I had installed* closed. The blinds you wouldn't even have if it weren't for me."

His eyes softened. "Look, Jane, it's been a long and tedious night. Can we not do this right now?"

She crossed her arms. "Not do what? Talk about the fact that I saved your ass tonight, and you won't even let me listen to the rain?"

"I just need some peace and quiet."

What the hell was his problem? "Oh, I'll give you peace and quiet. If you want to live your death like your stuffy, dusty, boring old attic, you go right ahead...but I don't want any part of it." She flung open the door.

He sighed, resigned. "Where are you going, Jane?"

"To dance in the rain." She marched outside and slammed the door behind her.

Peace. That man wouldn't know peace if it bit him on his cold, hard, very enticing, undead ass. And to think she'd actually allowed herself to fall for him, to *like* his uptight personality. *You've gone insane, Jane. That's all there is to it. Becoming a vampire has corrupted your mind.*

No more. She strutted onto the sidewalk, letting the downpour soak her to the bone. Tilting her head toward the sky, she closed her eyes and just *felt*. The fat droplets splattered on her cheeks and rolled down the contours of her face before sliding onto her neck, washing away her worries, as her mother liked to say.

The thought warmed her soul. Her fondest memory of her mom was dancing in the rain when she was five years old, splashing in the puddles and not having a care in the world. Mr. Broody McBroody Pants wasn't the only one who'd lost a loved one. Even after her mother passed, Jane still enjoyed a good thunderstorm, because it reminded her of simpler times. Of love and laughter.

Something she'd never get from Ethan Devereaux. She'd have to inform Gaston that the stake wedged up Ethan's ass had become a permanent fixture. She'd managed to wiggle it loose, but he seemed to like it right where it was. Another meeting with the Magistrate was in order. If she could get them to extend her biter's permit indefinitely, maybe she could get them to free her from Edward Cullen too. This vampire gig was easy peasy. She didn't *need* a mentor.

The front door opened, and Ethan appeared in the doorway. He hesitated there, looking up at the sky, shaking his head slightly. Jane ignored him and held her arms out to her sides, spinning in a circle before kicking her boot through a puddle, sending muddy water splashing across the walk in a wave.

He leaned against the door jamb, silently watching her until the weight of his gaze became too much to bear. She stopped her dance, parking her hands on her hips and returning the stare. He didn't budge, didn't open his mouth to speak, but if he wanted a standoff, he'd better have his big boy britches on. Jane was the queen of the silent treatment, believe it or not.

She moistened her lips and cocked a brow as his gaze fell to her mouth. His lips twitched before he pressed them together hard and looked into her eyes.

"It was storming the night Vanessa died. Rain has put me in a bad mood ever since." His eyes held pain and guilt, and her heart softened into mush.

"It's been twenty-five years. It's time to stop beating yourself up over it."

"I know. I'm sorry." He uncrossed his arms and let his hands dangle at his sides. No fists. "I'm ready to move on."

"Prove it. Come dance with me."

"Jane…"

"I'm a master of words, Ethan, and they go a long way. But real emotional connections between people happen because of actions. You can't change the past, but you can decide, right now, to change your future."

"It's forty degrees outside. If you were human, you'd be freezing."

"Well, it's a good thing someone turned me into a vampire." She held out her arms. "Dance with me."

His lips curved into a half-smile, and he stepped off the porch into the rain. "There's no music."

Thunder clapped in the distance, and she took his left hand in her right, resting her other hand on his shoulder. "Nature is its own symphony."

They swayed softly, and she inched closer as he slid his arm tighter around her waist. "Tip your head back," she said, and he obeyed. "Let the rain wash away your guilt, your pain. Make the decision to let it all go and be in the moment. To live your undead life in the best way a vampire can. To—"

"Hey, Jane?" He opened his eyes and locked his gaze with hers.

"Yes?"

"Shut up and kiss me."

"Now that's what I'm talking about." She crushed her mouth to his.

His lips were cold…because he was dead…but not in an icky corpse kind of way. Probably because she was dead too, and they were the same temperature. Despite the lack of warmth, they were soft, and as he coaxed hers apart with his tongue, she went all in, pressing her soft curves against his rock-hard… *Wow. And I thought his muscles were big.*

She couldn't help herself; she had to feel it. Working her hand between their sopping wet bodies, she grabbed a handful of cock, and sweet Satan's balls, it was *way* more than a handful.

He sucked in a sharp breath as a deep, sexy growl rumbled in his chest. "Ready to be impaled?"

"Fuck, yes."

He scooped her into his arms and carried her into the bedroom, tossing her on the bed like she weighed no more than a bean bag. She wiggled out of her shirt and threw her bra aside as he peeled off his clothes. The button on her jeans unfastened easily, but wet denim was like shrink wrap on a curvy woman, and she flopped on the mattress, lifting her hips and trying desperately to get the damn things off…to no avail.

Ethan stood there in his boxer briefs, Vlad straining against the fabric, and he smiled. Cheese-and-crackers, that man had a gorgeous smile. If her clothes had been dry, they'd have fallen off on their own. "Need me to help?"

"If you want access to the goods, you're gonna have to." She lay back and lifted her hips while he worked the fabric down her legs.

"Fuck, Jane, you're gorgeous." His eyes devoured her. He hadn't even touched her yet, but she felt like he'd caressed every inch with a simple sweep of his gaze.

"I like to think I can rock these curves."

"They're delicious." He licked his lips, and her center went slick. Good goat cheese, the man might make her come before he laid a finger on her.

Sitting up, she yanked his underwear down, freeing his dick, and man, oh man, had she hit the jackpot. She gave him a lick from base to tip…all nine inches of him…and sucked him into her mouth. He groaned and gripped her shoulders, letting her get in a good three or four strokes of her tongue before he pushed her onto her back and dove for her sweet spot.

Sweet baby Hades the man knew how to lick, but Jane hadn't gotten enough of his dick. She wiggled free from his grasp, using her vampire strength to toss him onto his backside so she could go back for more.

He was having none of it, lifting her and putting her right where he wanted her, but Jane knew a thing or two about wrestling. They rolled about, grappling—in an oh so sexy way—for dominance, until she got him on his back where her mouth could reach him and his mouth could reach her, and devil have mercy, that man had a way with his tongue.

He worked her into a frenzy while she sucked him, and as the most powerful orgasm she'd ever experienced exploded inside her, she was overcome with the urge to bite. His dick was in her mouth, so she released him and leaned over, taking in a mouthful of duvet and biting hard as she screamed.

With that need satiated, she sat up, removing herself from his face, and flopped onto her back. "Quick question. Do we have to worry about pregnancy or diseases?"

He chuckled. "We're dead. What do you think?"

"I think you need to give me everything you've got."

"Are you sure you can handle this much man?" He winked.

"Try me."

He climbed on top of her, filling her with one swift thrust, and stars danced before her eyes.

"Holy fuck."

He groaned. "It does feel a bit like a religious experience, doesn't it?"

"Take me to church, baby. Yes!"

He pumped his hips, and it didn't take long before another orgasm coiled in her core, ready to unleash like a river bursting through a dam. His rhythm increased, and as he shuddered inside her, her entire world flipped upside down and turned inside out. This man had a magic cock.

They lay still for a few moments—not catching their breath, since neither of them was breathing—but holding each other as Jane tried to figure out what the hell just happened to her heart. Sex had always been just sex, completely separate from love.

But what she and Ethan did was so much more than that…for her.

"Vampire sex is amazing," she whispered against his ear.

"Sex with *you* is amazing." He rolled off her, and she moved to her side, propping her head on her hand. Her lips tugged into a smile she couldn't have fought if her undead life depended on it. Ethan smiled too, melting her heart even more, and his gaze flicked down to her mouth.

His eyes widened, and he reached for her, running his thumb along her teeth. "Your fangs are coming in."

"Really?" She felt her mouth, and her canines extended into two tiny points. She sat up and looked in the mirror on the dresser, baring her teeth and furrowing her brow. "They're so much smaller than yours."

"They're not fully grown in, but it's a start." He folded his hands behind his head. "They look good on you. Very sexy."

Her stomach fluttered. "You think so?"

"I do."

"When we were going at it, the first time you made me come, I had this incredible urge to bite you."

Mischief sparked in his eyes. "Why didn't you?"

"Well, for one, your dick was in my mouth at the time."

He cringed.

"I didn't figure you'd want me biting that."

"Good call."

"Is that normal? To want to bite the man I..." She almost said love, but she *so* wasn't ready to go there. "The man I'm screwing?"

He chuckled. "I wanted to bite you too."

"Why didn't you?"

"I didn't want you passing out on me. You wouldn't have bled—vampires rarely bleed—but I was afraid even the act of biting would trigger you."

She lay beside him. "So, if I sank my baby fangs into your shoulder, even if I broke the skin, you wouldn't bleed?" Her mouth watered at the idea, which was beyond weird, but hey, she was a vampire. Who knew what was normal anymore?

"Do you want to try it?"

"You'd be okay with that?"

He gestured to his dick, which was hard already. "Just talking about it has gotten Vlad's attention, so yeah. I'd be more than okay with that."

She leaned down, softly grazing her teeth over his skin before nipping just hard enough to get a reaction out of him...and he reacted by moaning, tossing her onto her back and commencing a festival of biting and sexing that lasted until the death sleep pulled her under.

Two and a half weeks had passed since their first foray between the sheets, and Ethan couldn't get enough of Jane. Who knew vampire sex would be so hot? He hadn't allowed himself any form of pleasure while his guilt ate him from the inside out, but Jane… Jane had changed him. She'd changed everything.

He'd finally let go of his past and embraced his eternal death, and it was all because of the undead angel wrapped in his arms. He craved her with a ravenousness so much stronger than anything he'd ever felt. He needed her more than he needed blood.

She'd agreed to let him train her, and he'd bought the supermarket out of zucchini on more than one occasion, trying to help her learn the proper biting techniques. But her fangs hadn't extended past the tiny pricks that formed the first time they made love, so every time she bit into a squash, she tore the flesh with her incisors. She'd cause way too much pain for her donor, and though vampire saliva had medicinal properties, the gash she'd leave on someone's neck would require stitches to heal.

If she could just get over her aversion to blood, her fangs might fully extend. Her mind was holding her back, but he had no clue how to help her overcome it. Sophie had suggested Jane watch him feed, thinking since they enjoyed biting in the bedroom, she may enjoy watching him bite someone else.

Frankly, that made no sense at all. He also enjoyed impaling her, but hell would freeze over before he'd watch another man touch her. But he was out of options, so he tried feeding in front of her. Again, the moment his fangs met flesh, Jane either turned away, or if she witnessed the puncture, she fainted.

Feeding from a human and biting a lover during sex

were in no way related. And Jane was no closer to passing her test to receive her biter's license than she was a month ago.

Still, he couldn't fault her. As she lay next to him, her dark hair spilling over the pillow, he ran his fingers through the silky strands and pressed a kiss to her forehead. She was perfect. Exactly who he needed.

She smiled and stroked his cheek with the back of her hand. "I'm getting thirsty."

"Me too."

"Do we have any miracle cure left in the fridge? If so, we can stay in tonight, see if Vlad wants to come out and play."

"Mmm… As wonderful as that sounds, I'm afraid we're out. I'll need to at least make a run to the bank to restock."

A pounding on the door echoed through the house a second before Gaston's voice sliced through Ethan's mind. *"Get up, both of you. We have a problem."*

"Oh, for fuck's sake." He rolled out of bed and pulled on his jeans.

"That eye roll used to be reserved for me." She sat up and scooted to the edge of the mattress. "Gaston must be up to his shenanigans again."

Ethan slipped his shirt over his head and ran a hand through his hair. *"The devil himself better be here to claim our souls, or I swear to Satan, Gaston…"*

"He may be, my friend. Constable Watson's shown up with a directive from the Supernatural World Order. Every vampire must be licensed by tonight or die."

CHAPTER TWELVE

"I'll handle this. Don't worry." Jane patted Ethan's hand, and while he appreciated her attempts to calm him, he'd have preferred to hightail it out of Louisiana and never come back.

"I can talk circles around that weaselly constable. By the time I'm done with him, he won't know his fangs from his fingers. We've got this."

Gaston tipped back his flask of alcohol-laced blood, draining it dry before shoving it in his jacket pocket. "I'm truly sorry I missed your previous session. I hear you were quite impressive."

Jane straightened her shoulders. "I was on fire."

"This, I'm afraid, is a different matter," Gaston said. "A directive from the Supernatural World Order is binding. Even the Magistrate has extremely limited options."

"But he does have options."

Gaston sighed and looked at Ethan. "She's insufferable, isn't she?"

"She used to be." He kissed her on the cheek, and the door swung open. Jeffrey escorted them to the Council's chamber and closed the door, the lock sliding into place sounding like a nail in a coffin.

"Did he just lock us in?" Panic flashed in Jane's eyes.

Now it was his turn to calm her, though his own fear was evident in the crack of his voice. "It's…normal, right, Gaston?"

Gaston opened his mouth and touched his tongue to a fully extended fang. "Completely."

Constable Watson had dragged his baby throne from the side of the room to sit in line with the Council, and his beady eyes gleamed as he flashed a shit-eating grin. The Council members sat utterly still, their black robes engulfing their frames, and Ethan could finally see why Jane found them so amusing the first time she came in. The whole lot of them looked as if they'd stepped off an eighties B horror movie set.

His lips betrayed him, curving into an amused smile as they stopped in the center of the room to address the Council. Watson narrowed his eyes, obviously annoyed at the fear he failed to strike, and rose to his feet.

He unrolled a scroll—a fucking scroll…who still used those?—and read in a haughty voice. "The World Order of Supernatural Relations hereby decrees that all vampires within a one-hundred-mile radius of any populated city must be licensed to bite by seven p.m. this evening, or they will face the stake." He pulled a watch from his breast pocket. "Oh, look at the time. It's seven-thirty."

"What? No!" Jane stepped forward, addressing the Magistrate. "Sir, I have three days left. You gave me an extension. He can't do this. *You're* in charge here."

"Laws are laws, and this comes from the SWO." Watson rolled up the scroll and set it in his chair. "The Magistrate has no power in this case."

"Of course he does. He rules Louisiana," Jane said. "You're just a grunt. A messenger for the Order."

"Surely there's something you can do, Your Honor." Ethan stepped beside Jane. "She's a valuable asset." *"Precious,"* he added in Jane's mind, and she took his hand.

The Magistrate straightened, emboldened by their ego stroking, and turned to Watson. "I've read the directive, and I am well aware of my rights and jurisdiction." He turned to Jane. "Unfortunately, Ms. Anderson, my rights are very limited in this instance. I can grant you a one-hour extension. Find a donor, properly glamour them and bring them here for your biting test. Pass it, and you will be licensed and legal."

Jane's mouth hung open, and Ethan's posture deflated along with his hope. The glamour she might be able to pull off, but her tiny fangs would never get her through the biting test, even if she could manage to stay conscious through the ordeal.

She would never pass that test, and he couldn't live a single day without her. "Stake me instead."

"Are you crazy?" She whirled to face him. "You're not taking the punishment for my limitations."

He pulled from her grasp and stepped toward the Council. "Sir, if you keep her under your care as one of your own, surely the license won't be an issue. It's not her fault I turned her against her will. She shouldn't suffer for my sins."

"Keep me as one of his own? Like a slave? Oh, hell no. That's not happening."

The Magistrate steepled his fingers. "It is within my right to take a servant, whom I can do with as I please."

Jane paled.

The Magistrate continued, "Of course, Ms. Anderson,

I have no interest in women sexually, but you'd make a fine business associate." He frowned at Ethan. "I rather liked you, Mr. Devereaux, but we do need to send a message that things like this won't go unpunished."

He swallowed hard. "I understand, sir."

Gaston, standing off to the side, hung his head.

"No, no, no. Nobody's getting staked." Jane held up her hands. "When does my hour start?"

"Jane." Ethan reached toward her but let his hand fall to his side. "You can't pass that test."

She straightened her spine and shook a finger at him. "I love you, Ethan Devereaux, but don't you *ever* tell me what I can't do."

His heart swelled, feeling as if it burst in his chest. "You love me?"

"Well, duh."

Jane strutted up Esplanade Avenue, a woman on a mission, her five-inch stiletto boots clicking on the concrete with each determined step.

No way. No *fucking* way was she letting that weaselly bastard lay a claw on her man. If she had to eat a human's still-beating heart, she'd do whatever it took to keep Ethan safe. She paused, the mere thought of the bloody organ making her head spin.

She could do this. She didn't have a choice. Straightening her spine, she turned in a circle. "I know you're following me, Gaston. You can turn off your glamour."

His form shimmered in front of her before coming into focus. "You're getting good if you could sense me."

"I'm already good." Really, she hadn't sensed him, but

she knew they wouldn't send an unlicensed, fledgling vampire out into the night unescorted.

"What is your plan, Miss Jane?"

"I don't have one yet. Right now, I'm winging it, and for that I need a wingman…wingwoman. I have to talk to Sophie." They'd been in plenty of pickles together, and they always managed to talk themselves out of the mess. Aside from both her and Ethan's lives being on the line, this was no different. *Think, Jane. You can't stand to look at blood, so what can you do?* She marched up the front steps and threw open the door.

Sophie sat on the couch with a dark-haired man with brown eyes and buff shoulders. He was twirling a lock of her hair around his finger, but he jerked his hand away when Jane stomped into the room.

"Sophie, I need your help. You." She pointed at the man and thumbed toward the door. "Out. She'll call you later. This is an emergency."

"Yeah, I've got your number. I'll totally call you." Sophie stood and stepped around the coffee table. "Bye, John."

"It's James, but…" He screwed up his mouth on one side, glaring at Jane until Gaston stepped into the room. One look at the ancient vampire, and John-James scurried out the door.

"Well, hello, tall, pale, and gothic. What can a human girl do to help out a couple creatures of the night?" She paused and glanced over Gaston's shoulder. "Where's Ethan?"

"He's about to be staked if I can't get my act together and bite someone." She told her what went down in the Council chamber.

"That son of a bitch." Sophie crossed her arms. "If I

ever get my hands on the little prick, I'll kick him all the way to Alaska in the summertime. A little midnight sun will take care of him." She wrapped an arm around Jane's shoulders. "Tell me what I need to do."

That was the problem. Jane worked best under pressure, but this was more than her undead mind could handle. Ethan's life…err, death…was on the line.

She chewed the inside of her cheek as an idea formed in her head. "You're good at faking it, right?"

Sophie grinned. "Darling, I'm the master." Her smile slipped. "Which is actually kinda sad, come to think of it."

"If we get through this, I'll find you the biggest, burliest werewolf in New Orleans, and you'll never have to fake it again. I promise."

She narrowed her eyes. "Are werewolves any good in the sack?"

"How should I know?"

Gaston cleared his throat. "I have heard they exhibit quite a prowess in the bedroom. Nothing compared to vampires, I assure you." He smoldered at Sophie, but his smolder didn't hold a candle to Ethan's sexy stare. Besides, Gaston was *so* not her type.

Sophie gave him a once-over, as if considering his offer —*man, it must've been a while for her*—and then turned to Jane. "Okay, but I'm not doing it doggie style every time."

"I'm sure he'll do you any style you want, babe. Now, about my dilemma…?"

"Right. What am I faking?"

"I will try my best to glamour you, but if it doesn't work, I need you to pretend like you're hypnotized. Just stare straight ahead. Don't fall over yourself or anything, but…basically act like me before I've had my morning coffee."

Sophie went still, a blank stare filling her eyes as she dropped her arms to her sides.

"That's perfect." Four years in the high school drama club had served her friend well.

"Ah, yes…" Gaston cupped his chin in his hand as he examined her. "But at the moment of the bite…or pretend bite…you must react; they always do. An erotic moan won't work, as you're best friends. Try a quick inhale as you might do at the moment of *another* type of penetration." The poor guy was still trying to smolder at Sophie. He could have easily used his own glamour to make her want him, but then Jane would have had to kick his ass. Good thing he knew better.

Sophie sucked in a breath and even gave her body a little shudder, tilting her head slightly.

"Damn, that's sexy. You really are good at this." Jane grabbed her shoulder, giving her a shake to see if she could hold character. "We've got to find you a good man."

Sophie blinked, coming back to herself. "Tell me about it."

"I'm going to have to put my mouth on your neck, but I won't bite hard. You don't want to see the damage I've done to all the squash in New Orleans. Then I'll have to lick your neck to pretend like I'm closing the punctures. Stay hypnotized until we leave the building. I doubt they want humans knowing where their coven headquarters is."

"Jane…" Sophie took her hand, squeezing it tight. "If you have to bite me for real, do it. I'm down for whatever it takes to keep you and Ethan safe."

How the hell did Jane get so damn lucky? Aside from her current predicament, of course. She had the absolute best friend in the world, a vampire sex god for a boyfriend, and she'd stay young forever.

She pulled Sophie into a tight hug. "It won't come to that."

"Let's hope it doesn't." Gaston opened the door. "If you're not glamoured properly, the pain will be excruciating."

"Cheese and crackers, Debbie Downer, that was the least helpful thing you could say." She hooked her arm through Sophie's and strutted outside, glaring at Gaston as she passed. "No more negativity, Nancy, or I'll ban you from my club when it opens."

"Please accept my apologies, Miss Sophie. If you need someone to kiss it and make it better when she's done, I'm happy to oblige."

Sophie patted his cheek. "Thanks, Gaston, but I'll take a big hairy wolf over a cadaver any day. No offense, Jane."

She laughed. "None taken. Now, let's go get my man."

CHAPTER THIRTEEN

J ane stopped a block away from the coven headquarters and took Sophie's face in her hands. "Remember, if this glamour doesn't work, you're me first thing in the morning."

"Zombie girl. Got it."

"But not too zombie." Jane stared into her eyes, calling on her magic and focusing on wiping Sophie's mind.

Sophie froze, her eyes widening for a moment before she stared blankly in front of her, her lips parting slightly. Jane snapped her fingers in front of Sophie's face, and she didn't flinch. Either her friend's acting skills were top notch or Jane had gotten better at glamour. She didn't have time to worry about it, though. Her extension ended in ten minutes.

She guided Sophie into the Council's chamber, and her heart wrenched when she found Ethan chained to the wall, his arms out to his sides, exposing his chest. "Motherfucker." She started toward him, but Gaston's heavy hand on her shoulder reminded her of her mission. If she could get that damn license, all of this would be over.

"I put in a call to the Supernatural World Order," Watson sneered. "If you fail, you'll both be staked. Insolence will not be tolerated."

Jane fisted her hands to keep them from shaking—maybe that was why Ethan did it so much—and looked at the Magistrate.

He shook his head, his eyes apologetic. "The order comes from the Emperor himself. I've done all I can."

She straightened her spine, feigning confidence. "It's okay, boo. We got this." She winked and flashed a smile at Ethan. The sadness in his eyes nearly tore her in two. *You've got this, Jane. Fake it 'til you make it,* she said to herself.

Mr. Weasel Watson stood and brushed his trench coat back, giving Jane a glimpse of the stakes secured inside. What kind of a sadistic fuck carried around weapons, flashing them at people to exert his dominance? *A fuck with a tiny dick, that's who.*

"Proceed, *woman.*" Watson said woman like it was a bad thing to be one.

Misogynistic, sadistic, tiny-dicked fuck. Jane positioned herself in front of Sophie, looking into her blank eyes and searching for any sign of awareness. Sophie didn't even blink. She leaned toward her neck.

"You can do it, Jane. I believe in you." Ethan strained against his chains. "Just pretend it's tomato juice. You're sucking it right from the fruit."

She paused and looked at him. "Tomatoes are vegetables."

"They're actually fruit."

"You wouldn't put them in a fruit salad."

"And that's the difference between knowledge and

wisdom," Gaston growled. "You have two minutes, Miss Jane."

"Right." She looked at the curve of Sophie's neck and instinctively knew exactly where the vein lay beneath her skin. Her head spun, and she closed her eyes, placing her open mouth over the target.

The bitter taste of Sophie's jasmine body lotion battled with the sweet fragrance, and Jane focused on the disjointed sensation waging between her senses of smell and taste. She swallowed, but before she could pull away, the weasel shot to his feet and marched toward her.

"I'll inspect the puncture wounds before you seal them."

"Uhh…" Jane's voice was muffled against Sophie's neck. "There's no need for that."

"Oh, but there is." What was it with this guy's diabolical-sounding voice? You'd think the fate of the world hinged on Jane passing this test.

She licked Sophie's neck and straightened. "Oops. Already sealed. Sorry not sorry." She shrugged.

Watson glided his nose along Sophie's neck, inhaling deeply before glaring at Jane. "Lies! There's no trace of blood. No linger of vampire magic. This woman has never been bitten." He yanked a stake from his coat and lunged. Jane jumped out of his path, so he headed for Ethan.

"No!" Jane hissed, and her fangs extended fully, not because she craved blood, but because she would fight to the death for the man she loved. Sadly, fighting wouldn't help her in this instance. "I'll do it. I'll do it. Don't hurt him!"

The Magistrate lifted a hand, freezing Watson to the spot, and he rose, descending from his throne and approaching Jane. "You have thirty seconds, my dear, before I'll be forced to release him."

"Wow. I've got to learn that little trick." No wonder he was the man in charge.

"Twenty-five seconds."

Jane squared her shoulders, clutched Sophie by the arms and opened her mouth. Then she closed it again. The entire room spun, and her head felt so light, it might float away.

"Fifteen seconds." The Magistrate lifted his hand, ready to release his magical hold.

Oh, fuck it all. She sank her fangs into her best friend's neck.

Blood pooled from the wounds, and she created a seal around the punctures with her lips, sucking like her life depended on it—which, it did.

Really lightheaded now, she pulled away and looked at what she'd done to her friend. No ripped flesh. Sophie had barely reacted. Only two small holes marred her skin, and thick, red blood oozed from them, sliding down her neck.

Jane didn't pass out. In fact, she felt energized, and the blood dripping from her friend's neck had her mouth watering for more.

The Magistrate nodded. "Seal the wounds."

Jane licked Sophie's neck, and the sweet, coppery taste danced on her tongue one last time as the punctures sealed, leaving no trace of their existence behind.

"Mark her," the Magistrate said.

Jane held Sophie's head and claimed her as a meal, which felt odd as all get-out, but whatever. She'd done it. She'd drunk a human's blood, and it actually wasn't bad. "Did I pass?"

The Magistrate steepled his fingers, a small smile

curving his lips. "Indeed, you did, my dear. Well done." He bowed his head slightly and returned to his throne.

Gaston released Ethan from the chains, pulling him and Sophie aside as the Magistrate unlocked Watson. Jane laughed as the weasel stumbled, his stake sticking into the wall where Ethan had stood.

Watson hissed, baring his fangs as his pupils narrowed to slits. "I will not be made a mockery by a woman."

He unwedged his stake from the wall and lunged at Jane. The fucker was actually trying to stake her. *Bastard.* She feinted left, grabbing his arm and using his momentum to send him flying across the room.

As his feet hit the ground, he came for her again—*did this guy not know when to give up?*—and she spun around, delivering a back kick straight to his chest. Her stiletto pierced his ribcage, puncturing his heart, and he exploded into a pile of ash before her foot hit the floor. *Oops.*

"Holy shit! Remind me never to get on your bad side." Ethan took her hand and gaped at the mess she'd made of the weasel.

Jane looked up to find the entire Council and every member of the coven in attendance staring at her with wide eyes. The room went so deathly silent, you could have heard a mosquito fart.

As Ethan noticed the silence, he straightened and addressed the Magistrate. "She acted in self-defense, Your Honor. There's no crime in fighting for your life."

No one spoke. No one *moved* for a good thirty seconds, and Jane was just about to kiss her undead life goodbye when the Magistrate did his signature finger steeple and nodded.

"Indeed, she did, Mr. Devereaux." He looked at Jane. "The little bastard has been after my job since the moment he arrived. You've done us all a favor tonight, my dear. Jeffrey." He waved a hand, and Jeffery approached, presenting her with a credit-card-sized piece of plastic. "Congratulations, Ms. Anderson. You are now licensed to bite."

She looked at Ethan and wiggled the card. "I told you I had this."

He smiled and wrapped his arms around her. "I'll never doubt you again. Good job, princess."

She laughed. "Jane Anderson, Princess of Darkness. It has a ring to it."

"It certainly does."

"I'm going to need a prince, though. Are you interested in the job?" She slid her hands up his shoulders to cup his face.

He returned the gesture. "If it means spending every night of the rest of my death with you, sign me up."

She kissed him, using her magic to mark him, to claim him as her own forever and ever. He did the same to her, and the small hole she'd felt in her heart filled in.

He tucked a strand of hair behind her ear. "I love you, Jane."

"Words I never thought I'd hear from your mouth." She grinned and grabbed his ass, pulling him toward her. "I love you too."

EPILOGUE

Epilogue Seven Months Later

Ethan adjusted his black silk tie in the mirror and smiled at Jane's reflection behind him. She wore a deep red strapless ball gown with a full skirt and tight bodice that accented her delicious curves. She'd swept her long hair up in a twist with a few silky strands spiraling down around her face to accent her crimson lips. He'd never seen a more lovely sight.

Jane rested her hands on his shoulders. "Ready to go, Edward?"

He pressed his lips into a line, glaring at her.

"You're right. You're way too hot to be Edward. Louie? Lestat?" She tapped a finger against her lips before snapping. "I've got it. You're Elijah Mikaelson."

He turned to face her, taking her in his arms. "I'm simply a vampire."

"And I'm simply your victim."

"There's nothing simple about you, princess."

"Damn straight." She gave him a quick kiss before turning and tugging him out the door.

They'd worked together over the past seven months to organize and open New Orleans' first vampire bar, and the premise had been a hit from day one. Jane's social skills were unrivaled, and patrons lined up down the sidewalk and around the building for a chance to experience Nocturnal New Orleans at its finest.

Ethan kept the books, working five nights a week alongside his bride, living his death to the fullest with the most wondrous woman in the world. With her aversion to blood cured, Jane fed like a natural, and when she flashed her sexy fangs as they approached the club, Vlad sprang to attention.

He pulled her close. "We could skip the club and have a party of our own."

She bit his bottom lip, and his knees nearly buckled. "Let's save it for the after party. I promise it'll be worth the wait."

"You're killing me, woman."

"You're already dead." She nipped his earlobe before taking his hand and strutting through the entrance.

Sophie sashayed toward them wearing a black witch costume, complete with a pointy hat and broomstick, owning her ancestry though she didn't possess an ounce of magic to speak of. Gaston's meal mark glowed in her aura. "There you two are. I was getting worried." She waved her broomstick at them. "It's Halloween, not a formal ball. Where are your costumes?"

Ethan bared his fangs, and Jane turned her head, revealing two fake puncture wounds with synthetic blood dripping down her neck.

Sophie rolled her eyes. "A vampire and his victim? How original."

Jane snickered. "I'd like to know why you're wearing Gaston's mark so early in the evening. Is there something you want to tell me?"

"Yeah. You said there'd be werewolves here, and you promised to introduce me to one." She crossed her arms. "I was nervous. I can't tell which guys are checking me out because I'm hot and which ones are looking for a drink, so Gaston took a sip and marked me as a favor."

"How nice of him." Jane winked at Ethan.

Sophie glared at both of them. They could think whatever they wanted about Sophie's relationship with Gaston, but it would never go the way Jane would love to see it go. Gaston was a nice guy, and he and Sophie had become friends over the past few months, but despite his repeated offering of certain benefits, she couldn't imagine climbing into bed with a man who was as cold as a corpse.

"I can't tell who's human and who's a supe, so if any werewolves show up, you're going to have to point them out to me."

"Most everyone here is a supe. This is an invitation-only party, and just a few humans were invited." Jane linked her arm through Sophie's, turning her to scan the crowd. "Let's see. I'm not great at reading magic in auras yet, but I can tell you that good-looking guy over there is one hundred percent human." She turned some more. "What do you think about him? He's got a magical shimmer around him."

Sophie eyed the man. He was tall with broad shoulders, which she liked, but going on looks alone, he was blond. She preferred dark hair. "Hmm. The initial spark of attraction isn't there, but if he's a werewolf and a nice guy, he might grow on me."

Ethan leaned his head between theirs. "He's fae. Werewolves have an orange glow in their auras."

Sophie sighed. "Damn. I need a beer."

Jane joined her at the bar, though she had a glass of the "house red," which was really blood, and Ethan sidled next to his wife, sliding his arm across the back of Jane's seat.

"What do you know about werewolves?" he asked.

"Nothing. While you've been integrating your wife into the supernatural world, I went back to Texas to get that branch of my business running under new management, and I've been so busy since I moved here, between getting the new office set up and trying to activate whatever magic I may have inherited from my grandma, I haven't had much time to research."

"Why are you so interested in dating one?" Why did he care?

"Because they're part animal. They're wild and untamed." And Sophie had never met an animal that didn't like her. She had a way with them that astounded most people, and it was why her dog walking business had taken off so well. "I might even let him bite me if he has magical healing spit like y'all do."

Ethan shook his head. "Werewolves aren't allowed to bite other supes. It's part of the truce."

"It's a good thing I'm not a supe then. Sometimes I like it a little rough."

Jane snorted, and blood dribbled down her chin. "It's true. She's told me stories."

Ethan ignored their banter. "If a werewolf bites you, you'd better hope the only magic you got from your grandma is your scent. Otherwise, his magic will mix with yours, triggering the were mutation, and you'll turn into a wolf too."

"Oh. Ew. Okay, I'll do all the biting then." She definitely did *not* want to turn into an animal herself. "Honestly, guys, I don't know. There's something about a man who can turn into a predatory animal at will that's sexy as all get-out. You vampires are cool…too cool for my liking, and witches are bitches, so I've learned. I just really want to meet a werewolf."

"Oh. My. Goat cheese pizza." Jane gripped her arm. "The Magistrate is here." She slid from her seat. "I have to go welcome him. If any werewolves show up, Ethan and I both promise to introduce you, right, Ethan?"

"Sure." He stood and followed Jane as she sashayed toward New Orleans' most powerful vampire.

Sophie had another beer alone at the bar. Between having no magical signature in her aura and Gaston's meal mark making her off limits to the vamps, no one paid her any mind, except for her bladder, which, after her third beer of the night, demanded attention.

She slipped out of her seat, tipping the chair forward to lean the back against the bar, the universal signal for *this seat is taken,* and began the trek to the restroom. Two steps into the journey, her bladder decided she wasn't moving fast enough and threatened to soak her panties in a not-fun way. She practically did the pee-pee dance the next fifteen feet toward the door until a broad chest and thick, auburn beard caught her gaze, making her forget all about her problems down under.

Now here was a man she'd happily take home, whether

he was a werewolf or not. His golden-brown eyes gleamed the color of dark honey, and thick, wavy auburn hair matched his beard perfectly. His tanned skin said he worked outside, and that cop outfit. *Damn.* Whether it was a costume or he was an actual cop didn't matter. It would look amazing on her bedroom floor either way.

Her bladder protested as she altered her course, but it could wait a few more minutes. She'd never forgive herself if she didn't say hello to a man who could melt her panties off with a simple smile.

His devilish grin widened as she approached, and she licked her lips, taking in all six-feet, three inches of him. "Hi. You're a cop." She'd meant for it to be a question, but something about being near the man made her brain go haywire.

He chuckled. "And you're a witch."

She adjusted her hat. "Guilty. I'm Sophie, by the way." She bit her bottom lip, willing the sudden urgency of her bladder to ease so she could talk to the man.

"Are you okay?" Amusement danced in his eyes. "You look like you might be in pain." He gestured to her crossed legs, and she looked down, horrified to find herself standing in the classic little kid *I've got to pee* pose.

"I, uh…was on my way to the bathroom." Heat flushed her cheeks as she jerked her thumb toward the ladies' room.

"Do you need an escort?"

"I can make it on my own." She turned but paused, refusing to let her embarrassment get the best of her. "Will you be here when I get back?"

One corner of his mouth lifted into the sexiest crooked grin she'd ever laid eyes on. "If you're lucky."

"I always am. If you play your cards right, you might

get lucky too." Before he could respond, she tossed her hair over her shoulder and turned, using every ounce of control she could muster to stop herself from sprinting to the toilet.

With her ill-timed potty break complete, she adjusted her bra in the mirror, tugging her witch dress down just a bit to show a little cleavage. There was nothing wrong with tempting the man. If his personality was as nice as his looks, she'd be a sure thing. It had been months since she had a man in her bed.

Her excitement faded as she exited the restroom. The handsome cop was nowhere to be found. She scanned the club, skirting the edges of the dance floor and searching for a sexy man in uniform, but he'd disappeared. *Well, what did you expect, Sophie? The pee-pee dance isn't exactly a mating dance.*

She started toward her lonely seat at the bar, but movement in the courtyard caught her attention. Had her sexy cop stepped outside so they could talk in private? She could only hope. The door stood ajar, but as Sophie slipped through it, she found the enclosed park area empty. *Damn.*

As she turned to head inside, the bushes rustled in the back corner, and a whine emanated from the darkness.

"Who's there?" She glanced toward the door, but no one had followed, so she tiptoed deeper into the courtyard toward the movement. As she approached, the bushes rustled hard, and something in the corner growled.

She crouched down, peering into the dark shrubs, and found a pair of yellow eyes staring back at her. She couldn't make out exactly to whom they belonged, but the silhouette looked like a medium-sized dog. "Hey, buddy. Are you okay?"

Her voice should have soothed the beast instantly. She reached for the dog, but instead of coming toward her like most animals did when she spoke to them, it inched back.

"Come on, sweetie. It's okay. I won't hurt you." She scooted closer, her hand just a few inches from its furry muzzle.

The dog growled. Then it snarled. Then it lunged, snapping its jaws around her arm. Sophie yelped, falling back on her ass and clutching her arm as the creature bounded out of its hiding place and leapt over the fence.

"Goddammit, that son of a bitch bit me!" Blood dripped from the gashes, sharp pain stinging down to the bone as a strange tingling sensation shimmied up to her shoulder.

Jane ran to her side and dropped to her knees. "Are you okay? Let me see." She clutched Sophie's arm and examined the wound as if her previous issues with blood never existed. "Come inside so we can clean this up." She tugged her friend to her feet.

Sophie's shock turned to anger. "I own a fucking dog walking business, and I've never been bitten. Never. This is bullshit." She turned her arm, peering at the mark before looking at Ethan. "Did you see what kind of dog it was? I think it was a German Shepherd. We should call animal control."

"That was no dog." Ethan shook his head, his expression grim, though that wasn't unusual. Shoving his hands in his pockets, he glanced at Jane before focusing on Sophie, pity softening his gaze. "I hate to say this, but you've been bitten by a werewolf."

Crescent City Wolf Pack Series

Werewolves Only

Beneath a Blue Moon

Bound by Blood

A Deal with Death

A Song to Remember

Crescent City Ghost Tours Series

Love & Ghosts

Love & Omens

New Orleans Nocturnes Series

License to Bite

Shift Happens

Life's a Witch

Spirit Chasers Series

To Catch a Spirit

To Stop a Shadow

To Free a Phantom

ABOUT THE AUTHOR

Carrie Pulkinen is a paranormal romance author who has always been fascinated with things that go bump in the night. Of course, when you grow up next door to a cemetery, the dead (and the undead) are hard to ignore. Pair that with her passion for writing and her love of a good happily-ever-after, and becoming a paranormal romance author seems like the only logical career choice.

Before she decided to turn her love of the written word into a career, Carrie spent the first part of her professional life as a high school journalism and yearbook teacher. She loves good chocolate and bad puns, and in her free time, she likes to read, drink wine, and travel with her family.

Connect with Carrie online:
www.CarriePulkinen.com